SALutations!

Happiful Reflections of a Wonderful Life

A Collection of Essays

8/2/18

Dear Richie,

Read this for better health! I truly hope you enjoy my book!

God Bless!

SALVATORE GUARINO

ISBN: 0999818309
ISBN-13:9780999818305

Praise for *SALutations!*

"*SALutations!* gets to the core of the defining encounters that shape your life. Reading these passages brought me to the moments that broke me down, which became the very moments that formed who I am. The intricate details of family memories influenced by Italian roots brought tears of nostalgic joy to my eyes as I recalled my own upbringing in a lively Brooklyn-Italian family. Every story is hauntingly familiar and incredibly relatable to each and every one of us. Your first job, first kiss, first heartbreak, first understanding of mortality… each word will transport you to your past and make you want to call home and say thank you."

Christina Fontana
Documentary Filmmaker

"In a series of well written, touching, and memorable vignettes, Mr. Guarino thrusts himself upon the literary scene as a warm-hearted, New York, Italian-American, street-wise guy whose love for his daughters and the New York Yankees are unbounded. Some of his essays demonstrate a startling and honest self-awareness of his failed marriage and his acceptance that being a street hustler is part and parcel of who he is. A theme appearing in numerous essays is his unending search for love, lust, and romance beginning at age 12 and still appearing in his final and latest writing.

Stories from his childhood such as "Where's the Dog?" are hilariously funny, while others such as "How Old Are You Now?" and "Victoria Visits the YanYans," are heart-wrenching and emotionally inspiring. I found most of the essays enchanting and appealing to every little boy, teenager, divorced husband, and father who dwell within us. Although this is Mr. Guarino's first venture into writing, I hope that it is not his last."

Charles A. Moss, Ph.D.

"The books I have most enjoyed have transported me from the cacophony and tedium of the world around me to the place and time in which the story takes place. To do that successfully in a singular jump is quite a task. To do that repeatedly through decades and emotional highs and lows is nothing short of spectacular, and that is exactly what Guarino has done, in the smoothest of manners.

Salvatore Guarino's novel, *SALutations!*, took me on a ride which at times was an out-of-control roller coaster and other times as smooth as a 1979 Cadillac Sedan DeVille, listening to Mr. Frank Sinatra, as cool and relaxed as could be. Over a period of years, he masterfully weaves a tapestry of vignettes to give a glimpse into the person who is Silvio DiCristo.

DiCristo is an ordinary New York City-raised guy who, being raised by an Italian-American family, is the embodiment of a New Yorker that we all want to cheer for. Eventually, the varnish begins to tarnish, and in many cases, it tarnishes faster and harsher than others. However, you often see the tenderest and strongest examples of love as he deals with each of his daughters in different situations, or as he, his sister, and eldest daughter lock arms to sternly advocate for the matriarch, returning the dedication that she had poured into each of them over the years.

The vignettes are crafted masterfully by allowing the reader to drop in at different stages of DiCristo's life, all the while capturing the interest to keep turning the page. The reader is drawn deeper into the individual characters coming back to more clearly understand the situation they have been described in. You will cheer for, cry with, and be in tune with Silvio as his is a character and a life that will stay with you long after you put the book down.

One of my favorite examples is Guarino's use of the word "happifulness" and it is from this that I believe this work has been born, from the fact that as he recounts moments from the blissful to the anguished and whilst there is pain in some of these, there is also a man who has found contentment, has found satisfaction, has found what it means to be happiful in his surroundings."

Michael R. Newman
VP of International Sales

To my mother, Violet DiCristo Guarino:

Just So You Know

I wonder at times,
if when your evenings descend,
the depth of your influence
you do comprehend?

I imagine, if credited,
you'd say, "no, no, no!"
So I thought I'd illumine,
just so you know.

Today, I'm quite happy,
and have been for some time.
The cadence of "doe doe"
sounds loudly in rhyme.

My daughters are thriving,
though sometimes through strife.
With spirit and reverence,
they celebrate life!

The heartfelt pursuit
of my lady divine
has also been bountiful,
and soon will refine.

True friends I've attracted
on both coasts and between—
such wonderful gifts
of a life lived serene.

Enthusiastically imbued,
joyful life I embrace.
The roots of my essence
are easy to trace:

defiantly happy,
amused by *each* day,
hallmarks apparent
of Violet's Way.

Epic resilience,
a testament of will,
your love unconditioned
commands respect still.

A Christ-like acceptance
through injustice and all,
no matter life's bounces,
you still want the ball.

Uncanny perception
of *all* far and near,
the sharpest of wits
can only endear.

Four score and six years now,
you've put on quite the show!
The graced world the winner,
myriad gifts you bestow.

I know well the tough losses
you've had to endure;
yet beyond *any* moment,
of one thing I am sure:

the warm joy in my heart—
in *each* beat it does flow—
is infused from my mother,
just so you know.

Editorial Acknowledgements

Maria Susan Guarino, *Editor in Chief*: Your enormous contributions to all facets of this work have made *SALutations!* what it is. Thank you for your wisdom, candor, professionalism, and integrity. Your effort was the key factor in my dream of writing this book being realized.

Dean Julius, *Contributing Editor*: I am grateful for your keen perspective. Your input has added a necessary range of depth and balanced tone to the fundamental spirit and structure of this work.

Vani Rangachar, *Contributing Editor*: Thank you for meeting my trust with a humble and diligent expression of your skills and enthusiasm around this project. Your final edits were essential.

FOREWORD

Michelle Moore, PhD

"I should write a book" is a familiar quote I've heard coming from Sal's lips on more than one, two, or ten occasions over the many years we've known one another. These heartfelt statements typically came on the heels of a poignant recollection of a childhood experience, or a grown-up epiphany, or blessed "Aha" moment. I wasn't surprised. If anyone should tell their story, share their story, why not Sal? When it comes to being a storyteller, he's got that nailed. So, I knew it was bound to happen. What I didn't know, however, was that I would be a part of the process, a part of his process; and for that, I am honored.

Being vulnerable is when we are willing to open ourselves to another, another in whom we trust, who can either hurt or heal us, but its foundation is one of trust and hope. *SALutations!* speaks to being vulnerable at its very core.

Growing up an only child I learned to entertain myself, soothe myself, lose myself, in books. I read, and read, and read. Books were my friends, my confidants, my siblings, my sanctuary. When it was a snow day, and there were many in Canada, I read. When I was sick, I read. When my parents argued, I read. The words on the pages created a life in which I was safe and at home.

Later in life, because of many years in school, I still lived in books, but it was different, very different. I had to read, the choice wasn't mine, not completely. As a psychologist, I know that writing, journaling, the telling of one's story can heal many of the storyteller's wounds. "Emotional autobiographical storytelling" (sounds so clinical) is a way in which you share your own personal journey as a means to gain knowledge, insight, and help others. Words are powerful, they have the ability and strength to impact others, in a very positive way. The stories we share can be validating for others. To know you're not alone, that the experiences we have might be similar to those of others, and maybe, just maybe, there's another way for us to look at those experiences, those trials and tribulations, with a silver-lining, or at least with another lens.

Sal's story is a very personal story, an intimate story of one man's life. It is about the loving, expressive, intense, forgiving, and very Italian family and childhood that shaped his dreams. It's a story about the wonderful, sometimes very painful, but rarely benign life experiences that sharpened those dreams, and about the struggle to fulfill them. It is a story about a man's family, the relationships that last, and those that fade, and the pricelessness of those relationships. It is the story of an honest man.

Sal's offering to us, this gift from the heart, is a collection of stories that are real, honest, and familiar in a way that is both comforting and a little uncomfortable (like truth can be). Stories that inspire, and honor oneself and the values, and often conflicts, we all have within us. It teaches us to find the courage in the face of adversity, to face it square on, no matter the adversary, we will persevere, we have to whether we like it or not, the choice isn't really ours. But the way we look at things, our perception, that is a choice, that's one we have to own. "I should write a book!" Yes, you should Sal. And for that, as one who's been lucky to know this story, I'm very grateful.

Preface

In Frank Capra's Christmas classic, *It's a Wonderful Life,* George Bailey, a humble, huge-hearted, do-gooder loses his faith in humanity after being worn down by the tedious demands his insatiable desire to help others winds up placing on him. During the film, George finds himself in deep despair—literally on the brink of ending his own life—standing on the edge of a bridge, clutching his life insurance policy that values him, "worth more dead than alive." The heavens answer the prayers of many in Bedford Falls and send Clarence, his appointed guardian angel, to save him. Clarence does not seem like an angel in the traditional sense. He is old, stout, has no wings, and favors *The Adventures of Tom Sawyer* over *The Bible.* Nonetheless, Clarence intervenes by giving George, as he says, "a very special gift—the ability to see what life would be like if [he] were never born."

George moves from disbelief at the heavenly intervention provided by Clarence to a gradual and profound understanding. He realizes that that he truly does have far reaching, positive effects on the lives of many others, and, as Clarence reminds George amid his epiphany, "You see, George, you really have had a wonderful life." With renewed gratitude and love for his wonderful life, George is reunited with his family and numerous friends. And Clarence, through his transformative work with George, finally earns his angel wings after 292 years. In the idyllic, perfect Christmas-movie ending, George finds a note from Clarence in an edition of *The Adventures of Tom Sawyer,* left in his Christmas tree. "Dear George:" it reads, "Remember no man is a failure who has friends. Thanks for the wings! Love, Clarence."

I have watched *It's a Wonderful Life* almost every Christmas of my life, and many times between holiday seasons, starting from my boyhood when my father first circled it in the newspaper TV guide, suggesting I stay up late to catch it. George Bailey's goofiness, like when he says "Hot Dog!" every time he clicks the lighter in the drugstore, and young Mary silently whispering her secret affections into George's bad ear over the counter at the ice cream shop soon became comforting echoes of familiarity that remain close to my heart today. I caught the annual showing on TV, then graduated to a VCR tape as soon as it was available.

Timely doses of this heartwarming classic, along with a good pizza, served as the right emotional tonic for tough times, like my first experience living alone in an Upstate New York apartment immediately after my brother's sudden death. Listening to George's monologue about needing to escape the small town of Bedford Falls, I was repeatedly inspired to dream about what my next step would be. I introduced the movie to my ex-wife and two daughters. Though our family may have moved from New York to Texas to Florida, our Christmases always included the touchstone of gratitude embodied by *It's a Wonderful Life,* and my pride at impressing my daughters with frequent, boisterous imitations around the house—George, Mr. Potter, and

Clarence the Angel. “Merry Christmas, Mr. Potter!” I’d yell through the house as my two daughters giggled with joy.

When I found myself once again alone, in a small apartment in California, after a legal battle and testaments against my character from longtime friends, family, and close colleagues—feeling more physically and emotionally alone and disconnected than I had ever known—I watched George on DVD, listening to Mr. Potter tell him he was “worth more dead than alive,” and I saw him lose hope.

From a very young age, I have always strongly identified with George Bailey. In my most joyous and my darkest times, George’s character has brought me comfort. Although my life has, fortunately, never quite teetered on the brink as literally as George’s when he stands on the bridge poised to jump, I strongly admire his rekindled, spiritually amplified enthusiasm. I, too, treasure the opportunities, big and small, to send a little bit of my own “Bailey ripple,” as I like to call it, out into the world. In fact, the practice of this daily joy has become the main engine of my emotional, psychological, and spiritual well-being. I truly derive frequent, heartfelt joy from exchanging a few words in the line at the grocery store, or inducing a smile from the barista at Starbucks, who could perhaps use a break from being peppered all day for her sins—like not giving a customer the right kind of almond milk in their cappuccino. It is from this framework of practicing how a joy shared is a joy doubled that *SALutations!* flows.

I don’t offer a strict, chronological telling of these stories, or a “how to” manual on anything, per se. Similarly, I don’t think I have a corner on the wisdom market, or on how anyone should live their life. Heaven knows there are enough books of these varieties already out there. Instead, I offer reflections and stories.

George’s problem was not that he did not have a wonderful life—it was that he did not realize it. In my growing practice of gratitude, I hope that through the sharing of some of these experiences, reflections, and truths, that you, my friend, might gain some momentum in doing the same. Perhaps you may find some value in examining more closely the frames of your own “wonderful life,” and you’ll find a little extra jump in your step toward creating increased joy in the future, or be a bit less inclined to look back with regret, even if you don’t run screaming through Main Street of Bedford Falls as George Bailey did.

Salutation. [sal.yəˈtā.SH(ə)n/] n. rooted in the Latin verb "salutare," which means "to greet," and can be defined as "the act of greeting."

May you enjoy receiving my personal greeting of *SALutations!* as much as I have enjoyed offering it to you.

CONTENTS

Prologue

I would usually be at least slightly distracted by the parade of beautiful women sauntering on a sunny afternoon around the pool area where I live in Orange County, California. This day, though, as I lay on a lounger, propped upright at the corner of the large, rectangular pool near the hot tub, I was disinterested in what surely could have been a set for a high-end, swimwear photo shoot. I sat consumed by a much larger force than that of the string bikini.

A dozen emotions swirled in my heart at once; each had a palpable sensation and solitary voice of its own—a potent collage of sentiments. My flurried thoughts transformed suddenly into a buzz of *must's*, *do's*, and *don'ts*, combating my complacency, and negotiating over which would get to "go first" in influencing my subsequent actions. As I lay there at the pool, experiencing this unusual and somewhat manic burst of energetic spirit, I felt unable to steer the moment and provide the positive energy and clarity I needed. These growing, catastrophic leanings of my heart and mind won the moment and took center stage in my soul.

Sitting in my poolside chair, the sun beating down on my chest, gazing without seeing into the clear, blue water of the chemical-free, California-asshole-approved pool, I acknowledged pristinely—without equivocation to myself—that I, nearing forty-six years of age, was unhappy, frustrated, profoundly sad, alone, and essentially broke. At that moment, I felt like a burning debris pile, amassed with discarded beginnings, broken ambitions, and smoldering ideals.

I agonized there in my chair—watching two women near me laughing and lounging, ignoring their small dog yipping frantically next to them—over the raw truth that I was nowhere I had planned or hoped to be in my life at that moment. By almost all of my own measures of success, I was failing. I was divorced for about five years. I changed jobs four times in the four-and-a-half years since moving to California for a "great" job—which only lasted six months. I owed more lifetime monthly alimony (yes, lifetime!) than could ever be paid by a human, not to mention the arrears. Vices—such as impulsive gambling and alcohol abuse, which had been mostly at bay since adolescence—eerily reappeared, circling like vultures over a dying carcass. Finally, searching for a compatible partner, I had been on more first dates in the past four years than Adam Sandler's fifty. I felt arduously stuck between half-hearted regret of the former life I forfeited and a better version, which now seemed like a faint mirage that I only vaguely imagined living.

Beneath the painful drudgery of my morbid stream of self-deprecating conscience, I continued, thankfully, to hear another voice begin to emerge more persistently from within. A spirit of resilience, which had defined most of my earlier life, began to ring its bells of truth and hope, however faint, countering the oppressive shrieks of pity, whose cries had become tunes far too familiar. *Am I going to settle for being dominated by these feelings of emotional quicksand?* I thought. *Allow myself to remain a derelict vessel, now beached off the Pacific, devoid of its once-potent and loud New York engines? Will I prove right all of those who have secretly delighted in my downturn with their cowardly assassinations of my character?*

I needed to stop my spirit from its continued freefall over five years of mounting tumult, but I was scared at the sober prospect that my plight might not reverse its course, that I had perhaps already lived out my most exceptional years as an adult—staking a claim to a nice-sized piece of the American Dream for about twenty-five years, and now these possibilities might ultimately take an about-face—that I had perhaps squandered my best opportunities in life and was going to wind up as one of those people whose tales of woe engulfed them from head to toe, pathetically "getting by" in the years to come.

After a few more moments of reflecting on the terror of my emotional state and potentially morbid path ahead, I quickly stood up out of my pool chair and simultaneously ascended from my mental despair. I circled the hot tub area repeatedly like a hungry bear craving food. I didn't give two shits what I looked like or who noticed me. I imagined my actions were a bit scary for the onlookers of my intense, almost frantic preoccupation.

Fuck this! I thought to myself.

Not so fucking fast! I envisioned saying aloud to the broken and beaten-down side of myself that wanted to continue to pour gas on the fire of his misery. Like a boxer on the ropes, nearing a heavy drop to the canvas, I refused to go down. I fought back with a desperate flurry of thought and emotion. I allowed myself the freedom to admit that I didn't love my current girlfriend—or even like her anymore—and that she was actually one of the meanest people I had ever met. I realized how I took "open-mindedness" way too far in dating her. I felt angry, but energized now, blurting thoughts out loud and getting looks of concern at my apparent resemblance to a troubled soul off his medication. *Fuck them, too!* to whoever was watching me, I thought, daring to allow myself to continue bellowing hope from my flickering embers.

I knew somewhere inside that I could feel happy and peaceful again, regaining and even exceeding a sense of excitement and purpose in the life I had often experienced in earlier years. I realized then that I needed to revisit a recurring ambition that I had never embraced for a dozen feeble reasons—to write a damn book. The idea always beckoned me with an elusive promise that the undertaking itself—the catharsis, the reflection, and the tedium—might help me turn the corner and make some sweet lemonade out of a large batch of lemons. (Or as my daughter Victoria says, "Lemons out of lemonade because lemonade is gross.")

I never dared to attempt it, though. I figured I didn't have the time, wasn't articulate enough, blah, blah, blah. Finally, I intuitively sensed this endeavor would be a gigantic step on my road to salvation. I saw the first tangible rung on the ladder toward psychic relief, and I knew I had to grab it immediately—with both hands.

While putting pen to paper was a necessary beginning—an initial turning point, as opposed to continuing to mentally short-circuit around the possibility of failing in my efforts—I still found myself dizzied by self-doubt. In an effort to take an honest inventory of my abilities, I saw myself as a good writer at best, not a great one. I was a guy with street smarts, cagey, who knew his way around an adequate, unpolished, non-expansive lexicon. But I wasn't sure I could write a book. As I continued to "devil's advocate" the prospect on paper, I was struck and inspired by the growing enthusiasm and positivity I felt toward giving it a go. The mere consideration of positively engaging in such an effort produced a drop of intrinsic joy to my very thirsty soul. This was one of the first pivotal moments for writing *SALutations!* And more importantly, it helped me begin to understand how to work through my negativity, which was often habitually instantaneous, cunning, reflexive, and intermittently debilitating. By deciding to keep doing versus overthinking, a path finally began to clear for an enormous surge of undeterred excitement, confidence, and productivity.

Sitting back down in my poolside chair, I picked up my yellow pad and clicked my pen. Looking down at the page, I did not think. I did not plan. I wrote. My yellow pad has contained so many of my scribbles over the years—from Yankees' statistics to business brainstorming sessions, my weekly budget to my grocery list, and even drawings of the mystical “Drainland” for my daughters. It then became the platform for these essays.

Not That Bad

Fibs, Oprah, and Screwtape

At her place in Costa Mesa, California, sitting on an uncomfortable couch, feeling equally uneasy with my then-girlfriend Joy next to me, I found myself rationalizing that both the couch and my relationship with her were "not that bad." After a mediocre Saturday evening, we were spending Sunday morning watching "spiritual" shows. She was a social worker, fixing the world one case at a time. I was a former therapist myself, and for years somewhat of a de facto life coach for many friends and family. So we shared an interest in personal growth and helping others hit their potential.

Sitting in Starbucks, she would lament over her failed relationship with her ex-husband, who "couldn't allow himself to love." We struggled together with the heartache and guilt of divorce, with the failure of breaking a bond that was meant to be "forever." At night, we enjoyed winding down with a glass or two of wine and "real talk," as I like to call it. With my past in addiction counseling, I empathized as she told me about her strained relationship with her sister, who, after more than twenty years of battling alcoholism, still couldn't make amends or "get it right." I had found a fellow "helper." Like me, Joy was an idealist and an empath, and together, we could only grow.

Oprah's Supersoul Sunday was on tap, and she had a guest on named Pressfield. It was a typical Sunday morning with Oprah—she sat sipping lemonade with Pressfield, an older, smiling man, outside in two wood chairs, an elegant vase of sunflowers between them. Because it was Sunday, and they were having a casual chat outside, Oprah had her shoes off, letting her toes enjoy the grass. Of course, that Sunday morning with Oprah involved no mosquitos, uneven grass, or loud neighbors, and the yard contained only one large, beautiful oak tree. If they were really outside and not in front of a green screen, I imagine this would surely be the perfect Sunday morning for the soul.

This morning, Pressfield talked about his concept of RESISTANCE (which, yes, he capitalized) as an internal force working against individuals trying to make positive, life-changing strides forward. He explained that one's RESISTANCE increases in proportion to the magnitude of the positive ideas they are on the cusp of implementing.

Essentially, people trip over their own feet.

I have often experienced that the early morning hours bring a certain clarity to my mind. Given a chance, the brain sorts out some of the mental noise and rationalizations, which blend in more easily with the day's chaos. The early morning dew of the mind seems to usher out denial-ridden folly and replace it with refreshing pangs of simple truth. And, on this very plain Sunday morning, in the most ordinary of settings in Joy's living room, this phenomenon occurred. I found myself struck by a flurry of epiphanies too large, too messy, and too complex for Joy's uncomfortable couch to accommodate. I felt as if I were floating above her couch and Oprah and Pressfield in their wicker chairs on the screen, amid the drabness of Joy's dark and dated California home. While my thoughts and sentiments were overwhelmingly frenetic at first, they quickly congealed into the most purposeful sense of truth and direction I had experienced in years.

Pressfield's concept of RESISTANCE, which appeared logical enough on its face a few minutes prior, resonated in this moment with clear profundity. I identified with his description of being engulfed in the mud of my own troubling form of paralyzing self-sabotage—a state that I was fully mired in at that moment across many areas of my life. I felt mindful of how mentally, emotionally, and spiritually stunted I had become over the last few years, and how I desperately needed change.

As I continued to watch, I realized that Pressfield looked a bit like another old man I admired. I likened RESISTANCE to another familiar notion lying dormant in my mind—that of the "Screwtape," coined by C.S. Lewis in his book *The Screwtape Letters.* While Lewis's concept is more religious in nature than I necessarily identified with, the degree of cunning and cleverness with which the Devil attempts to win over his subject's mind and soul is especially poignant, and parallels what Pressfield described. This old man sitting on phony grass with Oprah was communicating the same message as the wily Devil, penned by an Anglican theologian in the early 1900s. It was the same message I communicated to my daughters when they didn't tell the whole truth: "Are you telling a fib?"

The fib was on me. That Sunday snapshot with Joy represented my overall state of being at that moment in time: deeply dissatisfied, yet yearning for much more in life, and noticing clear and frequent reminders of my frustrated status. I started to realize Joy's version of saving the world was quite self-righteous. Those mornings at Starbucks—as she sipped her nonfat, grande skim latte with unsweetened almond milk and extra foam—she complained constantly about how her ex's inability to love her was, of course, solely an unfortunate deficit in *his* character and completely unrelated to *her* lovableness. At the end of the day, those one or two glasses of chardonnay she sipped to "wind down" were really three or four. And although her tormented sister was twenty years sober through AA, Joy still fervently refused her sister's numerous, earnest attempts to right their relationship. Joy was not a helper. She was a judger. Our "real talk" was no more authentic than the set Oprah and Pressfield sat on.

I knew on a gut level that a richer existence, one I experienced intermittently in life, was still possible. It had to be. I was terrified of being mired indefinitely in a sad form of emotional paralysis and anxiety. I felt stuck in the muck with pervasive anxiousness and untapped potential. While fleeting happiness did occur, it was little match for a deeper sense of sadness and dread about never again feeling truly fulfilled. I intuited that I needed so much more from life. However, whenever I tried to rise above this eerie tide, my own "Screwtape" dialed up his defiance, thwarting healthier and happier outcomes. Thankfully though, something about that tediously mediocre Sunday, seeing Pressfield describe my state of being and recalling C.S. Lewis's artful and enlightening prose, revived my own desire to change enough to tip the scale positively. My sense of desperation and unease morphed into the foundations of a joyful and long-sought personal liberation.

Although I knew on a gut level that I had to move on, this potent revelation was countered quickly and insidiously. Screwtape beguilingly whispered in my ear as I watched Pressfield and ate tasteless granola à la Joy, *But not so fast! Don't be rash.* My mind sought to comfort me, but stammered with nagging rationalizations of Screwtape's interjection. Arm around Joy, I squirmed in an attempt to get comfortable on her couch. Neither effort of the mind nor body quite succeeded. I began to acknowledge my emerging intuition that *not that bad* was no longer good enough.

A Boyhood Fib

Sweet Smarts

At six years old, I approached "The Stoop" after buying Kit Kats at Tony's Candy Store, around the block from my home in Brooklyn, New York. I would typically buy four of them on a Saturday morning for fifteen cents each, sixty cents total. On random occasions, Nonna, my paternal grandmother in her mid-80's, would sit on a chair on the stoop outside the door to our house. She lived in the basement with Nonno, her husband and my grandfather. Being the stereotypical Italian-American grandmother of that time (speaking little English, pretending to speak even less, and not truly caring if she ever learned another word of it) she often played the role of gatekeeper as my siblings or I approached to enter. The required toll always came in the currency of information—a satisfactory answer or two to her broken English interrogation. In my case, the line of questioning centered around my merchandising skills and ultimate frugality. I guess I can't really blame Nonna, who grew up in abject poverty in the Old Country, and probably never fully grasped the relative opulence ("abundanza," as we called it) she witnessed in America.

"Whadayoo get?" Nonna asked.

"These," I replied, showing her my bounty of four Kit Kats adorned in their undisturbed, bright-orange sleeves.

"How mucha?" she interrogated with the steely graveness of an international border agent assessing my legitimacy for entry. This was my opportunity to reply honestly, as an honorable, Catholic schoolboy should.

"Sssooo I got . . . uhmmm . . . two for fifteen, four for thirty," I said, cutting their actual cost into a creative "twofer" price, which was half of the true total.

Nonna nodded her old, gray head in approval.

"Notta too bad," she said with a conciliatory expression on her face, the unmistakable equivalent to the gate being raised for reentry into my home, free to enjoy my smuggled sweets.

That was the first time I remember the simple, potent benefits of a well-crafted and masterfully executed fib. Sure, I felt about two percent guilty, as I slid off the orange sleeve of the first Kit Kat, carefully removing the reflective foil housing the four perfectly quartered, longitudinal sections of sugary goodness. Then again, even that minimal pang of conscience faded amid the buzz of happiness in my Kit Kat-infused brain. After all, if I had revealed the real price to Nonna, she would never have let me cross the border!

Everyone Cheats

A Texas Dust-Up

"I don't know Mr. DiCristo—that $510 monthly note is fixin' to be a bit rich for our blood. Let's see what else we can do," the man said to me with a pronounced Southern drawl and a less-obvious skepticism about the whole car-buying process.

"Please, Mr. May, call me Sil," I said. "Now, *rich*, you could not have picked a better word. Do you and your lovely wife really want to feel anything less than rich for the next decade, especially since you mentioned you do a lot of road trips together?" I smiled at his wife, who was twirling her big, blonde curls, chewing gum, and eyeing the loaded Honda Accord I had just taken them to test-drive.

"Just think about it for a minute. I extended my arm, my hand facing upward, toward the road adjacent us, adding a visual prompt to my grand invitation. "You and Mrs. May. Can I call you Sandy?" She nodded. "You and Sandy, rolling down I-35 all the way to Corpus Christi to visit the boys, cruising at eighty down the open road, the moonroof open, sunglasses on, wind blowing in your hair, King George booming on the multidisc player, with Alan Jackson cued up. A chance to pay yourselves back for getting the kids through school and all the other hard work you've done. Rich doesn't sound so bad, now does it, Jim?" Staring at him dead on, I ceased making any further utterances, honoring the ageless sales dictate of going silent after attempting "the close."

"Oh, babe, let's get the car," she pleaded with her husband.

"Darlin', I know it's nice, but we simply can't afford it," he answered, holding firm.

"Completely understandable. I appreciate how you don't wanna overextend yourself. But just work with me here a second," I pitched, feeling the sweat under my suit in the one-hundred-degree Texas heat, realizing it was now the psychologically opportune moment to make this deal happen.

"I want you and Sandy driving off our dealership with the perfect car. I understand you're not just taking home a pair of Levis; this is a big investment. That said, aside from sleeping, you are going to spend almost as much time in this car as you do in your own home, if you can imagine. Now, I can show you some other packages with fewer of the options you prefer, and I will be happy to take as long as we need to do so. But we already have the financing approved, and I think you will be more at peace in the long run taking home the exact car you just drove. You mentioned wanting to be closer to $400 a month when you first came in, and we are about $100 higher right now, but as we discussed, you'll save about $40 a month in reduced fuel vs. that Explorer you are trading in. So that gets us to about $60 away from getting everything you want. I hate to break it to you, Sandy, but you just might have to sacrifice drinking two lattes a week, which will knock off another $35 a month. So that would leave us at $425, only $25 a month higher, about 6% above your original number. You are 94% there. Take it home today, and I'll pay for your lunch at my favorite restaurant while we get the car prepped." He looked at me and grinned.

"Well, shucks, we'll take it!" he said, reaching out to shake my hand. Peering at me from under his cowboy hat, he asked, "Say, how did a Yankee like you end up down here sellin' vehicles anyhow?"

Kathy and I had been married for almost six years when the first A-bomb landed on our marriage. We had moved to Texas with our three- and four-year-old daughters a year earlier so that I could pursue a graduate degree in psychology. The plan was pretty well laid out. She would quarterback raising the kids and work nights tending bar while I studied psychology and interned. Four years later, we would return to upstate New York, where a coveted position awaited me in my field. We presumed it would be a grind, but one well worth our efforts. Though it was a big move—one far from all relatives, friends, and any semblance of good pizza—we felt enthusiastic about our family adventure in the Southwest.

I withdrew from the program less than a year later. The workload was intense and tedious, and I was immediately and deeply disenchanted by the formal study of clinical psychology, a field I had already fallen in love with from the inside out through lots of rich, albeit informal, firsthand experience. The zeal that had driven me passionately in this direction for almost a decade vanished, feeling like a sudden loss of blood. I knew on a deeper level it was right to bail out, but I still felt dejected, ashamed, and deflated at becoming the "one in ten" predicted to drop out after gaining admission among 300 applicants. My dream of becoming a clinical psychologist was over.

We decided to stick around Texas for a while before charting the next direction. The kids were in a groove and it wouldn't have been the easiest task moving back across the country anyway. Honestly, I also wasn't looking forward to what would have been more direct versions of expressed disappointment from friends and family if we returned, most of whom were already conducting the onslaught from afar. No one had the balls to say what they really felt about it either, which made their disapproval even more noxious in its cloaked and nuanced forms. My daughters provided the one welcomed exception: at the tender ages of almost four and five, they were just fine with Daddy "selling Hondas now because he changed his mind." They had no idea how comforting their lone chorus of naïve and beautiful cheers was for me. There were at least two cool breezes in the thick, June Waco air.

Things were not as unconditionally blissful between Kathy and me, though. She didn't miss many opportunities to convey disappointment with my jumping ship on Plan A. And I often responded harshly to her frowns, projecting the sting of my dropping out upon her, which only added gas to the fire of our joint discontent. In addition to her incessantly expressed concerns about what we would do next and "how could [I] just stop going to school?"—utterances that were barbed enough themselves to thwart whatever dimmed spirit of resilience remained in me—I felt the ever-present, lonely pain of her unstated disgust and growing disinterest. She resented that we were stuck in Texas and that our best-laid plans had gone awry. While I suffered through the ego-reducing reality of living somewhere I had no connection to, except for the now-failed purpose that brought us there—a Baylor dropout taking a job selling cars on a hundred-degree lot to locals who wondered what I was even doing there—I began to develop an even more dreadful sense of my depressing situation. The one person I counted on to remain present and loyal throughout the storm had begun to drift.

Kathy's dawn arrivals from another "shift that went late" became more the norm than the exception. The black, painted-on Spandex and scant bright-green top, tied off well above the waist, which she had to wear for work, went from necessary evils, which she wore almost apologetically, to visual battering instruments she grew most comfortable adorning herself in. When Kathy first worked at Rodeo House, she squirmed out of our apartment on her way to work in such a gaudy and sexy costume, somewhat embarrassed at having to don the get-up. But soon enough she fueled her growing fires of frustration and blame toward me by flaunting it as she exited nightly to her flirty place of independence. I remember her stating aloud one night on the way to work, "If you could just stop doing what you were supposed to do with school, then why should I have to 'be good' myself?"

I went through what I suppose is the usual torment one suffers in such a position. I often asked why she would arrive home at five in the morning when they closed the bar at two. I sought clarification from her as to whom "everyone" consisted of, those who seemed to always "go to breakfast" together in the wee hours after work. Dazed still from my own failures, feeling "less than" in nearly all capacities as a man, save for my role as father of two precious girls, I was too pained and raw to risk confronting her bullshit and my denial too strongly. I sensed my fragility; hence, I opted to continue pretending I believed her lies to both of us for the time being. At least I had the fantasy of a faithful marriage to hold onto.

Then, Kathy's older sister Taylor came to visit for a few days. I realized just a few hours after she arrived that this was far from a casual visit. She had been summoned by Kathy, who had conveyed her fantastic version of recent events, including how lazy and irresponsible I had become, and that she was at her wit's end in her efforts to deal with me. Taylor never liked me, and I wasn't a reciprocal fan, either. I suppose any chance of a potential positive connection between us died on arrival when we first met at her college graduation a few years earlier. She attended Femisap University in New England, which I dubbed "F.U." for short. The commencement address, chock-full of anti-penis hyperbole, was received outstandingly by the whole student body and all guests alike. Everyone stood dutifully in unison, offering a rousing volley of obligatory applause. Except for me. I sat on my hands, smirking blandly, sensing that I might be transformed from "Silvio" to "Silvia" in a poof had I even moved an inch to pay homage to such vacant pandering. Nevertheless, the fact that I was feeling so sad, hurt, and lost over our sinking ship, and because I did know that Taylor's intentions were noble, despite being filtered through a far different lens than mine, helped me remain open-minded to her intervention.

The kids already in bed and Kathy out flaunting herself at work, Taylor and I sat on the green futon in the living room of my family's apartment to talk. It was around 8:30 p.m. and at that time, our place always looked as if a Texas tornado, in the form of Victoria and Nora, had recently blown through, with only a basic attempt at rebuilding in its wake. In the midst of this lull between storms, Taylor began with an instructive tone.

"Sil, this *transition* of yours has really taken a toll on my sister."

"Yeah," I answered, feeling guilty already. "I know this certainly wasn't our plan."

"The thing is," she continued, not seeming to have heard me, "while you're out selling your cars, taking your time to figure out your next dream in life, Kathy is slaving away at home, raising your daughters, working full time at night, and then waking up just a few hours later to start all over again."

"Well, Taylor, I'm certainly not selling the cars for fun. I guess I'm trying to figure out what to do next," I answered, already knowing this wasn't going to cut it.

"And that's all well and good. So you didn't enjoy school. You got bored or stressed because it was too much. Now you want to try something else. Whatever. But what about *her*, Sil? You need to help her. The thing is, *marriages* don't often go as planned. They are hard. They are work. And, unfortunately, you can't just quit working at your marriage to try to figure out what to do next in life. You know, Sil, even using that dominant language of '*I* am trying to figure out what *I* am going to do next' is enabling the very patriarchal, gender-normative, societal oppression that women have been battling for centuries. Contrary to how *you* may have been raised and to how society has continued to raise *you*, your marriage should be an *equal* partnership."

Ay, I thought. Her treatise on female oppression and role subjugation was quickly bringing flashbacks of F.U. to my mind.

"I know that this has been really hard for Kathy. I quit graduate school. We're living across the country. And I have been real moody. I realize *I* have a lot to work on. But, Taylor, I am pretty certain that Kathy is cheating on me. She comes home hours after shifts end. She goes out for breakfast with her coworkers, but comes home hungry. I mean, how do we move forward with this going on?" I asked, hopeful that perhaps my tormented heart and mind would gain some relief via these disclosures.

Taylor cut me off quickly though, interjecting with a slightly assertive yet matter-of-fact tone.

"Everyone cheats," she dictated. She stared into my sad eyes and through them to my already broken heart. Shocked by her words, and equally puzzled at the casualness by which she delivered them, as if informing me on the fact that water boils when heated, I froze a moment and ogled at her and her unnerving claim.

Did she already know something, I wondered, and was she merely attempting to normalize the excruciating truth I had been arriving at? Then again, Taylor had just recently "gone through something" in her own marriage, which involved sharing a naked hot-tub dip with her guru. So why should I have gauged any moral relevance from a person who viewed cheating as a rite of marital passage anyhow? I dismissed the idea that she possessed inside info quickly enough, figuring that Kathy would probably lie to her, too.

Taylor's words that followed for the next several seconds became a blur of passive sound, giving way to the hum of my own thoughts. I struggled to orient myself, feeling the instant fading of the brief and naïve hope of attaining some soul soothing from Kathy's man-hating sister. I felt the profound depths of my horrific aloneness plummet further, as if I were suddenly an anchored weight at sea. I didn't know where help could come from, but I knew at that instant that talking further with Taylor was no more useful than a boy trying to outrun his shadow.

"Everyone cheats," Taylor's smug words echoed in my mind.

Not everyone, I thought to myself, feeling an eerie sense of moroseness envelop me, further weakening my battered soul. *My wife surely does, though.*

Two Loaves of Bread

A Trip to Pete's

It was hardly past 5:30 in the evening on a winter night in Brooklyn. I was six years old. It was dark outside, and the house smelled amazing, as it always did that time of day, since my mom was cooking dinner, which we routinely ate at 6:00 on weeknights. I looked forward to eating dinner every day, and it always tasted like perfection. Ma would never make only one thing. Typically, there would be two courses, such as spaghetti marinara followed by chicken cutlets, pasta e fagiole, then fried eggplant, peas and macaroni as the opener for gravy meat, or escarole and beans as a prelude to meatloaf—Italian (with red *gravy*) or American (with ketchup), both were dizzyingly tasty.

As dinner drew near, however, my mother suddenly realized that a necessary component of the meal had been overlooked. We had run out of bread! In our house, bread was synonymous with eating, dinner, food, delicious, necessary, and wonderful. Simply put, bread's presence was essential. That's when my mom summoned me to save the integrity of dinner's sacred ritual. She clearly and directly articulated my mission.

"Go to Pete's and pick up some bread," she said.

There was no need for mention of additional variables, such as how we needed the bread for dinner, or that dinner was at 6:00, or that it needed to be "Italian" bread. Those data points, which might be necessary for a six-year-old in one of those "American" homes, were superfluous redundancies in our family. I eagerly embarked on my journey, one dollar in hand, happy hunger in my stomach, and a sense of unstated—yet unmistakably high—importance.

A block and a half and about three minutes later, I was at Pete's buying Italian bread, warm from their oven, loosely wrapped in its familiar white paper with the heel of the loaf peeking out from the open end—the red, green and black print denoting the brand, ingredients, and the price of thirty-five cents. While happy to save the day, I also felt a bit embarrassed transacting at the counter, because I was sure that Pete and Lucille, who ran the store, had realized Ma had run out of bread, which bordered on recklessness, if not sinful behavior, on her part.

I headed back down 14th Avenue a half a block, and then readied to turn down 40th Street to deliver the requested loaf. The winter air was cold, but refreshing. I held the bread tightly against my chest, as if it were a bag of hundred-dollar bills. The warmth of the bread, and its sweet, yeast smell seemed to bind with my cells on a molecular level. Knowing I was on the return route of my mission induced a self-satisfied air of well-being. I was proud of my efforts, so I rewarded myself by breaking off a nice chunk—a part of the loaf for the walk home. My pace began to slow to a carbohydrate-induced stroll.

About ten minutes later, right around 6:00, I entered our house, and before even removing my coat, I presented the loaf to my mom. Rather than looking pleased, as I had anticipated, she looked puzzled. She held the whittled-down piece of bread, which began its return trip from Pete's as a full loaf minutes ago.

Curious, she asked, "What happened?"

Slightly confused, but figuring she didn't appreciate my taking liberties with how much I already ate, perhaps exceeding what was customarily tolerated when buying bread, I sheepishly replied, "I ate some."

She broke into one of her famed bouts of laughter, laughing without sound for several seconds before gasping for breath like a baby having a good cry. Her curious gestures were immediately replaced by a look of understanding that could have served as a parental exemplar on how to convey the deepest empathy in seconds. She wasn't upset that I ate as much as I did. After all, she understood that I was essentially powerless over that gustatory action. Rather, she was asking what had happened to the second loaf I was supposed to buy. She got such a kick out of how I didn't realize that one loaf—well just over half of one loaf now—wouldn't be enough for dinner, which made my liberal gnawing even funnier.

Truthfully, my mom's approach to raising us was pretty tough overall, which was the norm in our culture at that time. But, on the occasions that really mattered, she displayed her wonderful and benevolent mastery at conveying a sense of acceptance, warmth, and forgiveness. That's exactly what she did then, thanking me for going to Pete's and not focusing on the one and a half loaves that never made it home. When the seven of us ate a few minutes later, no mention of my bread blunder was made. This was a big relief for me, as my older siblings would have taken advantage of the ready-made opportunity to mock me, the youngest of the five kids. It was no problem for my mom to cover my oversight anyway. She sliced off the rough edge of the remaining piece and quickly produced some "back-up bread" from the freezer (not having such a reserve was unthinkable), which she heated up so fast that it seemed like she performed a feat of time travel. And, through the years, those were the kinds of timely improvisations Ma always conjured in defense of my emotional well-being, making lemons into lemonade (or my preferred twist—lemons into limoncello), especially when I needed her to.

The Game

One Time! Just One Time!

At the sophomoric age of twenty-two, I accidentally stumbled into the most rewarding career of my life. For about a decade beginning in 1990, I worked with a private, residential high school in the middle of nowhere in Upstate New York. It was a boarding school primarily for teens who struggled with a variety of problematic behaviors.

I was privileged to work as a math teacher, group and family counselor, and as needed, a sports coach. Given the small size of the school, the staff often wore many hats. Most of my coaching was at an informal level. I would throw together a softball team, which would practice on an uneven, rocky field during the seasonable months, and we played a handful of fun games against the staff at the nearby summer camp, or the residents at a Job Corps facility in the area. These games, and an annual game against the school alumni, constituted our schedule, and despite the lack of formality, I helped teach students about camaraderie, having clean fun, and playing to win through softball.

As the school's enrollment grew, although still quite small at about eighty students, one of the kids asked me at lunch, in front of the entire student body, why we didn't have a "real basketball team" instead of playing three-on-three on an improvised court in an old barn. I thought seriously about my answer. My initial reflex was to convey the impractical realities of our situation: our small size, lack of adequate facilities, and the rigorous demands of the academic and therapeutically oriented schedule. After all, we didn't even have a gym in which to practice, no less to play, basketball. Then again, the school's mission was based on overcoming adversity, focusing on how one could accomplish a goal versus emphasizing the potential obstacles that existed. Sensing the weight of many eyes, ears, and hopes ready to rationalize how a staff member was about to give an excuse for why something was not possible (when students were taught twenty-four-seven that excuses were essentially bullshit), I replied that this student's question was a good one. I would look into the plausibility of having our own basketball team, and assured them I'd get back promptly with an update.

Two days later, I reintroduced the topic to the entire student body. Even though we had no gym, only three boys who had ever played organized basketball (none of them within the last year or so), only about ten students who had any ability to play even minimally well (and I do mean *minimally*) and no coaching or athletic director experience among the staff, I had enrolled us as an independent, high school boys basketball team—Class D in Section 9 of New York State. And I took my barely average, three-on-three skills from the playground in Staten Island to the coaching and athletic director ranks at the high school level.

Basketball was not known for having especially strong programs in this region; however, there were several highly competitive teams around with long, successful histories. Some of the programs had had the same coaches for decades, and all of them were well organized, established, and had one key advantage: a home court. The best we could do was agree to play all of our games on the road and use our neighboring summer camp's semi-enclosed, concrete court for practice. This was in Upstate New York's winter months, so despite my creative strategies to stay warm, such as having the team jog a couple of miles to the court for practice, it was still frigid.

Since we enrolled as a team after the regularly scheduled games were already slated that year, I scheduled all of our games for our first year directly with the athletic directors of schools in the area (and some way out of the area, too), filling in their schedules at their convenience. As one might imagine, they were elated to have this new and utterly novice team visit their courts for what would likely be lopsided contests.

I bought some coaching books—one from Bobby Knight on how to play a man-to-man defense, and one from "Coach K.," who espoused more of the model of coaching decorum and team organization I hoped to implement. I also visited the athletic director from Sullivan County Community College (a perennial force in Junior College hoops at the time) to ask for some fresh ideas on how to teach these ten boys with hardly any experience to play in the smartest way possible. He gave me some food for thought, and was cordial and supportive. As we discussed how David should position himself for the many Goliaths to come, he also seemed impressed that I had the *cojones* and foolishness to take on this endeavor. His body language conveyed his belief that we had no chance in hell, despite his best attempts to play it cool. A few weeks later, with maybe fifteen frigid practices under our belt and one scrimmage against a local team on the books (it was not pretty), we were "ready" for our first game. I had scheduled us in a tournament about two hours farther upstate. The schedule pickings were slim, but we were eager for our two-game, four-team, weekend tournament. We opened on Friday night and would play in either the winners round or a consolation game the next day.

Three minutes into the first quarter of game one, the other team—let's call them "The Big Guys"—whose smallest player was as tall as our tallest, was winning 12—2. I can still remember the looks in the eyes of my kids during the first timeout. They were shocked, dizzied, embarrassed, scared, mad, and exhausted. And they saw some of the same states of mind reflected in my eyes, as I uttered some strategy-based direction, which must have sounded how Charlie Brown's parents did to the Peanuts' kids. We lost 83—28.

But our consolation game did show one bright spot: We scored twenty-five percent more points than the night before. For those not great with numbers, we scored only thirty-five in total, but a coach can rationalize, right? The other team? Well, they scored 100, which is pretty hard to do in thirty-two minutes at any level. They even dunked on us midway through the fourth quarter, which served as an apt image to depict the sentiments around the whole weekend. Our eyes were opened. We were truly out of our league.

After a grueling van ride home that night and some cold practices the next week, my resiliency as a coach—now I felt official after receiving two rather legitimate beatings on the court—and the determination of my handful of boys were starting to percolate. "Z," the kid who had asked the question about starting the team originally, asked us all at a practice that week if we were going to be embarrassed again at the upcoming tournament. This was to be held at SCCC, the aforementioned college, which meant that it at least would be on a neutral court, and most of our student body could come to watch. Given the athletic director's interest in our enthusiastic mission, it felt a little more like a home game. Even so, most of the kids were unable to muster an equally optimistic tone in response to Z's attempt to rally us. Emotions aside, we worked hard at practice for the next week and started to show signs of organization, and more importantly, hope.

We played Eldred to open the tourney, which had the same two-day structure as our first tournament. Eldred's coach was the star player on the basketball team about twenty years earlier, and despite not having a vast talent pool in his small school, he did a great job of making the playoffs annually and getting his kids to routinely play over their heads. We struck up a small chat before the game, as our teams ran warm-up drills. He praised us for entering the league and making the best of a challenging situation. As we talked, he only needed a few seconds of observation to see the skills exhibited during layup drills by his team were far superior to ours. I remained undeterred and played it cool, as if I didn't notice this was likely to be another blowout.

I decided we should play a man-to-man defense because we had some athleticism on our starting five. And rather than give our opponent a chance to use their advantage in experience to exploit a zone, we would try to keep the game as close as we could to a playground style of play. We surprised them early by contesting shots and making some steals, and feeling for the first time in our existence like we might have a chance. *Maybe this whole basketball team idea wasn't a crazy notion after all.* These collective thoughts were a fitting metaphor for the life experience these kids had—"the same old, same old" defeats perpetuated by negative, self-fulfilling patterns of thought. Then, as had begun to happen in their lives at the school, a counter-thought, a swell of enthusiasm, began to emerge—a maybe, a *"what if?"*

After hanging around on the scoreboard into the third quarter, we amassed a lot of fouls due to our aggressive defense and were forced to shift to a zone. They shredded it in typical, well-disciplined, Eldred basketball fashion, and we lost by fifteen points. All in all, though, this was clearly our best showing, and even my cynically prone kids were encouraged. I could at least conduct a coach's postgame handshake that was not heavy with the weight of embarrassment.

The rollercoaster of a day started with our burgeoning enthusiasm taking an early and fast hit. The consolation game was against Livingston Manor, another well-established and well-coached team in the Hudson Valley of New York. We fell behind early, and we were playing flatly. Being new at feeling any kind of positivity on the court, as we did the night before, we lost our focus and quickly were down ten points. A player on their team scored his thousandth point of his high school career during the first quarter, which prompted a stoppage of the game and a brief recognition of his accomplishment. On one level, I appreciated what this kid had done and the need to recognize it, but the bigger part of me on that day had had enough of seeing other teams' successes on the court. We sloppily and lethargically played out the first half and were down around fifteen points at the break.

I tried my best to appeal to my boys in the locker room, reminding them that our fans were here in support, that the least we could do was to go out with a solid effort. A few bells were rung from my stirrings, but the pace stayed about the same for the third quarter, as the deficit grew to twenty-one points at the end of the frame: 65—44.

The students watching were growing disinterested, and, honestly, I felt disappointed, especially after last night's glimpse of promise, as I sat down on the bench for perhaps the first moment in all of our first four games. Typically, I would pace back and forth, locked into every play. Seeing my dejection, one of the school's owners walked down from the bleachers, and briefly sat on the bench with me between quarters. I fibbed and told him I was fine, wishing internally that I had the extra oomph to at least try and spur on the boys. I felt guilty for being so bummed out at that moment, but I was also paralyzed at the thought of breaking out of my mood and showing some serious heart, regardless of my wounded pride. For the moment, I remained seated and made the final quarter's round of substitutions in an emotionless manner. I figured I would give the starters an opportunity to at least make a good showing, so I sent Z in at point, Horns at shooting guard, Lance at small forward, Kareem at big forward, and Mac in the middle. Before they left the bench, Mac tried to inspire the team. He was a 5-foot, 10-inch football player from North Carolina—white as can be—with red hair and freckles, and he joined the team mostly because we needed bodies. And he figured it was better than being on the sideline watching. Mac was an enthusiastic, friendly kid, but generally, he had a quiet and humble demeanor. Somehow, here in the final quarter of play, he started barking at his teammates from the bench.

"What are we gonna do?" he yelled, his face flushed, red hair frizzing. "Just lose? Well, I'm not! We have the whole friggin' school right over there and all the players from last night filing back in for the championship game after ours with their fans, too—and they're all watching. This place is packed, and I wanna at least go out in the best way possible. Who's in?"

His four peer starters had to reply. While some were still whistling in the dark in terms of how they really felt, they all circled for a final "One, two, three, Falcons!" I felt a bit ashamed as it took Mac's call to arms to get me back off the bench, but I never sat back down. We went to tight man-on-man and a full-court, man-press defense. There was no reason to conserve any energy at this point. In fact, it was our one potential advantage. We went on a quick, eight-nothing run, our first positive jolt of the day, after a couple of backcourt steals and some end-to-end layups from Z and Kareem. We cut the lead to thirteen with a little under six minutes to play. The opposing coach called a timeout, which was a sensible move after our run. But no one in the building, himself included, thought the impossible was possible. He gave his boys an earful about finishing strong out of respect for the game, not in fear of losing it. Regardless, our fans started to chant "We Are Family," (the nickname of our school) echoing Sister Sledge's 1979 hit and the Pittsburgh Pirates' championship anthem. Our friendly athletic director was calling parts of the game over the PA, and he was helping stoke the fires of a potential comeback, including playing the actual hit song through the speakers.

The crowd started to get excited as they continued to chant, "All my brothers, sisters, and me!"

A few of the players from last night, who had come to play in the final, stayed to watch. They delayed entering their locker rooms in preparation for their own game. The truth is, we were still well beyond improbable as far as actually making this game interesting, but so many people—perhaps each for their own reasons—wanted the miraculous to happen and were beginning to sense that it might. The kid who was honored earlier, silenced our run with a quick jumper, bringing their lead back to fifteen, swishing the crowd to a rapid silence. That silence, however, was to be short-lived.

Our boys were not to be denied, it seemed. They pushed the ball up court, set picks, found the open man, and hit shots. When they missed, they stormed the glass and put in second-chance buckets. They pressed in the backcourt, forcing several steals and turnovers from traveling violations. Everyone blinked, and with under a minute to go, we had cut the lead to two points.

One time! I thought to myself with the ferocity of a degenerate gambler rooting for his horse down the stretch, imploring God to reward these kids for their pride-leveling leap of courage. *Just one time!*

Everyone was standing. "We! Are! Fa-mi-ly!" they yelled.

The building was packed, and it would no longer feel OK leaving today with only a good effort in hand. We needed to win. The other team advanced to the 3-point line and looked to take a good shot that could potentially bury us, increasing the two-point margin as precious seconds elapsed. Z, the kid who started this whole magnificent and improbable journey with his feisty and challenging question about starting the team, darted out from playing his man and stole a cross-court pass. He pushed the ball forward and ran it down-court. He was fouled on his way in for a would-be layup. Then, he sunk two glorious free throws, tying the game at sixty-five, and setting the stage for the other team to have a last shot with sixteen seconds left. We had scored fifteen straight points and twenty-three of the last twenty-five!

"I got all my sisters with me!" The crowd yelled, growing wilder in a nail-biting end to the game.

They called timeout to set up a final play. We discussed what we all knew was coming—a clear-out for their best player and earlier honoree. We decided Kareem would stick with him, and we'd maintain man-to-man coverage, being careful not to lay too far off the four other players in case they had a Plan B option for one of them. Play resumed. Honoree dribbled past midcourt and killed a few seconds off the clock, looking to drive and take a final shot with about five or six seconds left on the clock. If he missed his shot, they would still have a chance to score on an offensive rebound, leaving us almost no time in any scenario.

In what can only be described as an incredibly intense, eerie, and anxious moment, the crowd fell silent. Then, Honoree advanced toward the foul line from the top of the key, slicing into the top of the lane with about seven seconds to go. As he prepared to bring the ball up from his dribble to shoot, Z leapt away from covering his man and bolted into the side of the lane, once again deflecting the ball. Lance grabbed the ball and began galloping down for a breakaway score. He crossed the half-court line.

Four seconds left. Then the top of the key.

Three.

Brought the ball up to shoot.

Two...

...and was tackled by a sprinting player in a last-ditch effort to stop him from a certain, game-winning layup. It was properly called a flagrant foul, which meant Lance would get two shots *and* we would get the ball for the remaining 1.8 seconds.

While I didn't want to risk "icing" Lance by calling a timeout before his free throws, the hysteria now breaking out on and off the court necessitated it. I gathered the team, five panting horses with animalistic sweat and instinctual singleness of purpose.

"GET UP EVERYBODY AND SING!" our fans continued singing.

"*When* Lance makes his shots, all we have to do is inbound the ball, and we win!" I told them.

The cheering and singing stopped as a deafening silence once again overtook the gymnasium. Lance calmly stepped up to the line to change at least eleven people's lives forever.

Swish.

Our fans exploded. Their coach gasped. Their kids bowed in disbelief, even the ones on the court. The periphery of people around the court clapped, sensing the enormity of this occurrence on so many levels. It was sacred for these kids—they truly left it all on the court and took back with them a treasured memory and gargantuan lesson of a lifetime.

I thanked God at that moment and continuously in the postgame euphoria that consumed the locker room. There were no cell phones yet, so I called my wife from a payphone before leaving the gym. I had to tell her right then, even though we were only a short drive away. When I hung up the phone, I turned around, sensing someone was there. Patiently waiting to greet me while I waxed enthusiastic on the phone for several minutes was the opposing coach, who had lost what was certainly one of the most deflating games in his school's history. He shook my hand and offered a humble gesture of congratulations.

"What did you say to get them going like that down the stretch?" he asked me.

"Nothing. I just listened."

Snow in Waco

"But It Might Snow, Right?"

Our daughters Victoria and Nora were turning four and three already. It was the summer of 1996, five years into my marriage. The Italian twins, as I used to call them (so close in age to be Irish twins, but clearly Italian based on their eating skills) were the kernel of energy and attention within our young and busy family life. My wife and I raised our daughters in a very loving way, yet also more firmly than most. We weren't as preoccupied as some parents with trying to cushion all their falls in life. However, our hearts were as breakable as any parents' when it came to our daughters' potential hurt, especially when their most sincere hopes were on the line.

We moved to Waco, Texas, that summer from the Hudson Valley in the lower upstate region of New York. I was admitted to a graduate program at Baylor University, so we relocated. The kids welcomed the great trek, and they were excited by the prospect of having pool time for many months of the year. As Christmas approached, and the weather remained warm, the girls, already steeped in the wonderful habits and contagious enthusiasm that blow in with the snowy chill of a white Christmas, began to wonder when it would get cold and snow.

"When Nana and Gofather come to visit for Christmas, there will be snow just like in New York at the old house!" Victoria asserted one morning at breakfast with the air of a teacher conveying a well-established, indisputable fact, such as eight times eight is sixty-four. Her astute childhood intuition was also at work, signaling her to take note of some cues contrary to her claim. There was a hint of doubt in her otherwise-instructive tone. Victoria and Nora, via the fact that Victoria was the gatekeeper of her younger sister's expectations, remained hopeful that Victoria's wintery forecast of events would be as certain as the times tables.

I remember watching Victoria hold court that morning, a breakfast-time ritual, from the head of the kitchen table opposite me, her diminutive frame kneeling on her chair, adding a few inches of projective power to her presentation. She gave voice to a constant stream of busy, happiful thoughts, hundreds of tidbits and updates all in about twelve minutes. Nora sat dutifully between us, choosing practically to focus mostly on her Cheerios rather than attempt an interruption. Between slurps of milk, she curiously pivoted her head of long, unbrushed, brown hair alternately toward her sister's morning address and my facial reactions to Victoria's speech, widening her already-large, owl-like eyes. Victoria pointed her index finger at me, Nora, and the world, as necessary, amplifying her palpable, organic enthusiasm as she provided more information than the morning news shows, all from the most relevant source to her and Nora—Victoria's mind, of course. She outlined a review of our daily agendas, including the lead bulletin of whether Mom or Dad was to prepare dinner that night and what would be served. She was sure to announce how Nora was "still a baby," and thus played with the "little kids" at the daycare they attended, unlike Victoria, who was in the "big kids' class," among other headline news. As Victoria proceeded with her mostly upbeat Cheerios briefing, rife with editorial ad-libs, I knew that the emerging conflict about snow on Christmas was going to be a recurring story, and one I needed to consider weighing in on.

A big believer in shooting straight with my kids whenever possible, I was hard-pressed to be truthful about the upcoming holiday-weather realities without popping their winter balloons in the warm Texas air. After doing a little research on the possibility for December snow in Waco, and deliberating on whether I would employ preemptive truth or allow the eventual disappointment to naturally occur, I decided to break the news. The next morning at breakfast, they listened keenly to my multistage, boom-lowering, holiday-weather truth, wide-eyed and with utter disbelief visible in every facet of their adorably innocent body language.

Victoria, the chronologically inherent spokesperson for such pivotal matters, asked simply and in a uniquely assertive, questioning tone, "Yes, but it *might* snow, right?"

As if God had delivered this beautiful and timeless reminder right to my soul and brain, I instantly realized two things: that I needed to handle this one more like the mystery of Santa, letting nature and time eventually sort out the magical with the practical, and that Victoria's claim actually was 100 percent correct—it *might* snow. Acting on this welcomed moment of fatherly intuition, I smiled and looked reassuringly at the four brown eyes needing to witness unequivocal confirmation of Victoria's logically magical premise.

"Of course, it might!" I said.

And, a few months later, on a beautiful and magical morning in late December in Waco, Texas, in 1996, to the absolute and unbridled joy of two girls from New York, it snowed for the first time in twenty years. It was only a fraction of an inch, dust on the sandy dirt. And, as quickly as my daughters burst outside that morning with high-pitched giddiness to verify that their frosty wish had indeed come true, they returned to the cozy comforts of Swiss Miss with mini marshmallows and their third watching of *A Little House Christmas*. The amount of snow the girls witnessed, or how long they sloshed around in it, didn't matter, of course. The magic of this Christmas would be measured by the infinite delight that possessed my girls on that day. Their sweet and improbable hopes rewarded, the only people happier than they on that unlikeliest of days were their parents.

Just Throw a Ringer...

Sacred Time

I was seven years old and playing horseshoes with Eddie Patrillo, my summer neighbor in Sag Harbor, New York. Eddie was almost two years older than me and a pretty athletic kid, so I was always at a bit of a disadvantage as we filled summer days and early evenings with fevered games of horseshoes, badminton, frisbee, catch, and whatever else we conjured up to fill about twelve hours a day, winding down with the magical sound of the Ice Cream Man, whose musical truck might as well have been a chariot from heaven. Its harmonious chimes signaled the final prize at the end of an already fun-filled day. These were the innocent, carefree days of childhood, where a sense of warmth and well-being was the baseline of emotion, amplified even further by icing on the cake in its actual and figurative forms. Years later, my brother Gerard and I would coin such warm-spirited, serendipitous moments as "sacred time," a happiful concept I have always treasured.

The way we played horseshoes then, the closest shoe would get a point, two points if it were a hanger, and three points for a ringer. We set victory at 21. This one morning I was losing 20-18, and we prepared to toss the next two shoes each. After Eddie threw his set, and I had one left to go, we could easily see from the other end that he had the closer shoe. He was poised to tally another win in what became a summer sports-training league for me.

As I prepared to throw my last shoe, my two oldest brothers, Gerard and Joseph, came walking up to the edge of the wood fence dividing our yards. The horseshoe pits were set up in Eddie's yard, which, now that I think about it, gave him an additional edge, a home-field advantage.

As big brothers do when their little brother is involved in some head-on competition with a neighbor, they waltzed up to the fence with a cocky and cool indifference. They were, after all, too smooth at seventeen and sixteen to admit that they were interested in their kid brother's horseshoe match.

"What's the score?" Gerard said, without forsaking his coolness.

"Twenty to eighteen," Eddie chirped in response, gleaming in anticipation that he would claim victory after my final toss. My brothers saw his shoe sat in a winning position, only a few inches from the pole. Their body language suggested I was poised to lose the match, even though they pretended not to care.

"All you need to do is throw a ringer on this toss, and you'll win," Gerard said, likely driven by a sense of older-brother, obligatory encouragement.

Secretly, I wished that just this once, the horseshoe gods would concur with Gerard's directive and I'd pull off a miracle. I also felt a palpable sense of annoyance with Eddie's face shining with premature pride, which was amplified by the powerful fact that Gerard and Joseph were watching. Let's face it: even winning the next five games (after their brief interest waned) wouldn't stack up against doing so in this moment, which felt like watching Monday Night Baseball in our living room on WABC. I couldn't allow myself to resent Eddie, though, or to ponder how magnificent a miraculous toss would be. To do so would distract me from focusing on my final shot.

I locked in mentally, stood slightly to the right of the pole on our end and focused on the distant pole with a stare as intense as Superman's X-ray vision. Everyone was quiet as they paid homage to my rite of sportsmanship—an understanding that all boys inherently seem to know. My little arm swung back with the shoe, and with bated breath and the hopes of a million kids wishing for their older brothers to see them make their mark, I lunged forward and threw my horseshoe, along with my desperate hopes, into the summer wind and blue Sag Harbor sky.

And would you believe it? In what seemed like three hours of desperate and improbable longing, the horseshoe came angling in from the right, spinning with divine radar. It whipped around the pole. A Ringer! It stuck in the dirt with a violence and improbability only matched in degree by the skipping beat of Eddie Patrillo's humbled, broken heart. None of us could believe it at first, so we ran down to the far end to make sure that the horseshoe held its place in the sandy ground. And it had! Even Gerard and Joseph were shocked by my throw's accuracy. They tried to play it off like they weren't hustling to the other end of the pit to see my winning toss, but we all were.

On that glistening, sunny Sag Harbor morning, I beat Eddie Patrillo in horseshoes 21–20. I shut out his game winning point with the shot of my seven-year-old life. And most importantly, my big brothers saw it, sealing my place in the Little Brother Hall of Fame. I think I jumped up and down in celebration for half an hour. Eddie's premature gloats were reduced to silence and frowns. And that was OK with me. As my brothers strolled away, after my victory parade began, Eddie frantically insisted on several rematches, all of which he probably won that morning. It didn't matter. I won the biggest game, the one that Gerard and Joseph came to watch, and Sil threw the ringer of his life. It doesn't get more sacred than that.

And if It Were *Your* Daughter, Mr. Principal?

A Father's Resolve

My oldest daughter Victoria stands at about 5 feet, or maybe 5 feet, one inch, if she's the one providing the data. Her stature is really the only small thing about her, though. She's sweet, smart, divinely resilient, wise, and almost always happiful. The word "happiful" is her creation, in fact, and it's fitting because, like the word's intended definition, a new entity is also needed to truly articulate how one small person can contain and exude so much pure love in her small and beautiful heart. So one can only imagine how exceedingly irate I became when I learned that Victoria (then a fourteen-year-old, first-year high school student) was being harassed by an eighteen-year-old, 6-foot, 200-pound man (also a student) in one of her classes.

"Oh, there's the Jesus freak again! Did you say your prayers yet today, freak?" Man-Boy Goon mocked Victoria as class was dispersing. He was still seated and spewed his verbal bile as Victoria walked by when exiting the class.

"Leave me alone!" she snapped, swiping in frustration at his sketchbook, which lay on his desk, thrusting it to the floor.

"You're gonna pay me for a new one," he threatened, as he picked it up and pointed to the resulting tear on its cover.

"No, I won't!" Victoria shrieked, looking a foot above herself at his dark, cold eyes, pale skin, and inexplicable hair, which was molded into numerous spikes that jettisoned out from his head in a crown-like design, causing him to resemble a mutated Lady Liberty from the neck up.

"If you don't get me a new book by tomorrow, I am gonna fuck... you... up!" he countered, following her out of the classroom and then placing his gelatinous, oversized frame in front of her within an enclosed alcove that needed to be navigated in order to exit the room. He repeated this threat and other discontented grunts at her small and now-shaking personage, a mere half his weight. Victoria squirmed her way out of the vile and unintended shared space, frazzled and tearful.

As often happens with bullying, Victoria (the victim) was reluctant to tell her mother and me that he was bullying her. I learned later that day that Man-Boy Goon had been abusing Victoria for weeks, with one form of verbal assault or another, and that this particular incident was just the straw that had broken Victoria's back. His revolting collection of hateful deeds was repeatedly bullying Victoria for being openly Christian, short in stature, and "weird" through daily taunts and other abusive language. So, when Victoria finally shed light on his despicable and ongoing violence—most notably on that day's boisterous and direct threat of imminent harm—I knew it was time for some immediate and forceful action of my own.

The class where the recurring incidents occurred was in the afternoon, and I drove Victoria to school early the following day. We arrived at 6:30 a.m., forty-five minutes before regular classes began. I had her wait in the hall outside the administration office while I went into full Italian-father mode, channeling my inner Vito Corleone to assure an effective, overtly unemotional delivery. Being from Brooklyn, as well as living a life with more than its share of edge, has its advantages. Specifically, being able to convey a quiet-yet-unrelenting strength with a hint of "this guy's not gonna leave until you act" was as second nature to me as reading a Yankees' box score or twirling spaghetti without a spoon.

I asked the secretary if Mr. Dang, the principal, was in yet. She said he was and continued to say something about how I could set a time to see him depending on the issue, etc. Her words faded into the back of my senses like the static from my Uncle Mickey's television set when left on one of those in-between channels. I listened for less than a second, and then proceeded to make a beeline for Mr. Dang's office with a casual and matter-of-fact smile to the gatekeeper, who already gave me all the information I needed—the location of the soon-to-be-schooled principal. I entered his office and simultaneously made eye contact with him, seated behind his desk.

"We need to talk," I announced calmly and simply, taking an uninvited seat on one of the chairs facing him across his desk to state my case. Mr. Dang had impressed me before with his apparent genuine interest in his students and what seemed like a good-hearted manner, an impression that helped me enter his office with the benefit of the doubt still in play. However, I also sensed from him, within seconds, an air of suspicion of me. To him, I was an "I-talian" from New York, sitting uninvited at the desk of a man whom I perceived as a thick-necked, football-supporting, Central Florida-residing, "good-ole-boy"-turned-administrator. I momentarily forced myself to detach from my projection of his prejudice and proceeded to explain that my daughter, petite as she was, was being physically threatened by a student years older and literally twice her mass, a student who had promised to "fuck her up" if she didn't meet his arbitrary, bullying demands (essentially to kiss his ass) prior to that afternoon. While he was noticeably surprised at my unedited candor and sternness, he stuck to true principal form—unemotional and methodical—as he began to stoically shovel a pile of bureaucratic horseshit in my direction.

"OK, Mr. Deee-Christ-oh," he mispronounced. "I understand your concerns, and I will be sure to look into this and get back in touch with you after I make the necessary inquiries and gather all of the facts. Where can I get a hold of you later today?"

Mr. Dang stood up from behind his desk, taking a couple of steps toward the door, a leading prompt for me to do the same, and thus adjourn our impromptu meeting. Dang's dismissive and unsuccessful attempt to send me on my way, as if I were a nagging student griping for a schedule change, revealed his utter failure to appreciate what he was dealing with: the potency of fatherly conviction that had initiated this sunrise conference and anchored my indignant and fixed position in what had now become *my* chair.

I remained unmoved. I leaned back in my chair slowly and calmly, stretched my arms behind my head, a nod to the fact that it was still friggin' early and that I didn't pay him this important visit for an early dismissal. Tilting my head and fixing my eyes in a blatantly pronounced manner on three framed photos on the wall above his desk, which he now stood uncomfortably several feet away from, stranded from his feeble attempt to ring the bell early.

"Those your kids?" I asked, with a feigned buoyancy of amiable interest that a casual acquaintance might have earnestly brought to this exchange under more cordial circumstances.

"Yes, they are," he reluctantly bristled in response, signaling that he was beginning to grasp the tenets of today's lesson plan.

My Brooklyn instincts now asserting full control of my delivery, I asked him simply, with a slowed cadence and steely stare, "Would you *wait til' later* if it were one of your kids?"

I allowed the booming truth of the momentary silence that followed to ring in his ears for a few seconds. I continued, providing him with some additional facts of my own, a friendly headstart on the data he mentioned earlier he would have to gather. "I'll be staying here until this situation is handled, just as you would, of course. And, if it isn't handled thoroughly today, I will be making a call to WESH TV to shed some bright light on today's events in time for tonight's broadcast."

I did move to a new chair in the hallway outside the administration offices, my one minor concession to allow Dang to carry out his now-urgent business. I observed parts of the process unfold. First the Dean of "blah blah blah," followed by the "Liaison Between Misbehaving Students and the Legal Authorities" entered the building. And then, in all of his unseemly spiked hair and slovenly demeanor, entered Man-Boy Goon, looking as revolting as Victoria had described him. He was unaware of who I was as he was ushered passed me into an office to be debriefed, and I wasn't officially allowed to know who he was, of course, due to "confidentiality." Thankfully, though, my insistence on sticking around and making things happen now, not later, provided me the benefit of laying my eyes on him. It took only one second to make him a permanent resident in my memory, and I was pleased about this, in case the formal proceedings fell short and "other methods" of resolution became necessary.

As it turned out, Man-Boy Goon actually was not even registered for the class that served as his bullying grounds. He visited daily to spend time with his female goon, which was allowed by an incompetent and weak teacher. The matter worked itself out, since Man-Boy Goon knew he had been exposed—and I think he had a hunch I knew who he was. I am by no means a violence-leaning person, but if this issue had persisted, I wouldn't have hesitated to let the fruits of justice bear as they may have. I knew with every fiber of my being that I would protect my daughter as needed. I followed a natural law that supersedes all others, an honest, powerfully divine truth. And for me, that is quite sacred.

Alabama Bound

When Father Knows Best

About two years after I split with my ex-wife, in February of 2011, I was sitting on my couch in California one evening doing what had become the usual—mindlessly watching TV while scrolling through photos of Newport Beach's best surgical, cosmetic work on Match.com. Both activities, and the perfunctory way in which I carried them out, echoed the blues I felt. I could hardly make the partial alimony, and I truly didn't feel the sense of optimism that had been a pretty reliable and guiding instinct through most of my life.

Then Nora called me. As a good father does when his daughter calls, especially from across the country, I instantly perked up to the reminder of something bigger than my mortal woes and answered. Unfortunately, Nora's tone was anything but upbeat. She explained with an angry and frustrated barrage of words how she had just finished playing flute at a community concert event and waited to speak with the conductor, an accomplished musician and teacher whom she admired. She was dejected and hurt by his comments. Nora was finishing high school, and had become a truly superlative flutist, targeting colleges where she hoped to study Performance Flute. So, when the conductor asked her what plans she had on tap for next year, she excitedly conveyed her ambitions, along with some universities she had in her sights. Rather than share in her enthusiasm, he matter-of-factly dismissed her plans as naïve and commonplace. He remarked that "[she] and a million other flute players [would] be doing the same thing."

Although Nora is a quick study and had learned some tidy lessons recently about the utter rudeness that often accompanies professorial types, she also has always been the most sensitive person within a mile. His thoughtless utterance, along with his inconsiderate manner of delivery, really stung. What made this more difficult was timing. Nora was about to travel to the University of Alabama for a four-day audition in the Honor Band. This was one of those deeply collegiate traditions where nearly a 1,000 kids play in an elaborate series of performances, and admissions and scholarships are determined through the events. So it wasn't exactly a shot in the arm to be rudely belittled by a mentor.

Hearing her recount this incident and the palpable hurt and pain in her voice, the dad gene was activated and expressed in a rather stereotypical Italian-American manner.

"You know what, Nora?" I snapped indignantly. "*Fuck him*! He doesn't know who you are, or how special and talented you are. It's time to refuse any and all forms of negativity regarding how you play, and that's that! You go to Alabama this week and you kick ass because you are great and have been ever since you first heard the flute in church at ten years old. The fact that *he* is underestimating *you* has *nothing* to do with how successful you will be!"

I added a sacred story of my own about beating the odds in a former career endeavor to bolster my already bodacious pep talk. And, beautifully, I helped to point Nora's spirit in the right direction, which was, "*Fuck him*!"

"Wow, Dad!" she exclaimed. "That's awesome. I didn't realize you got that job on Wall Street at only twenty years old. And, yeah, you're right about him. Thanks!"

Twenty minutes and one wounded, redirected heart later, Nora was off to Alabama to give it her all, and I, in California, was given a brief, divine reminder of the things that matter.

Less than a week later on a Sunday afternoon, I was shopping for chips and other Super Bowl items to bring to a friend's place for a get-together. Ironically, it was my birthday. Nora called when I was in the store, and it was a good thing that I happened to have kept my sunglasses on. Before I could utter a full, "Hi, pal!" Nora burst into a joyous rant.

"Dad! You're not gonna believe this. I was doing the Honor Band all week, and on Saturday, they announced a few smaller scholarships for a bunch of kids. I was bummed because I didn't get any, and I knew I was better than them. But one professor asked me how to pronounce my last name, which I thought was weird, and I was hoping for something good to happen. Then, in front of like 1,000 kids and a whole bunch of parents, they said that one student—*just one student*—was being awarded a full, four-year-scholarship, less room and board, *Nora DiCristo*!"

I actually staggered, leaned against the row of chips, tears filling my eyes, and asked her calmly to please repeat what she said. I wanted to make sure, because I knew (but had not told her yet) that had she not gotten a scholarship, I hadn't a realistic clue on how we could have afforded her college. She repeated her unbelievably wonderful account, and added some cream to the cannoli by telling me that although she always calls Mom first for stuff like this (a practice I encouraged out of respect to her mother), she wanted to call me first this time because it was our phone call earlier in the week that made the difference.

Similar to my experience a decade and a half ago, when I was feeling lower than low about dropping out of graduate school, the pure and beautiful tones of Nora's enthusiasm once again struck the right chord in my troubled soul. Her infectious expression of joy in her accomplishment, and her crediting me (two time zones and countless miles away) with helping to bring it about, reminded me of how important the vast, unfinished symphony of my life still was, at least to my flutist daughter.

Come on, Ron... Have a Heart!

Things That Matter

It was February of 1979. I was only eleven years old, and my parents were soon to take me, my brother Paul (twelve), my sister Carmela (twenty-two), and my grandparents (on my father's side) to Miami for a long-planned, two-week vacation. Unfortunately, I broke my arm in a sledding accident a week or so before we left, so a cast above the elbow limited my activities some. Dad had a fabulous surprise in store, which, given my misfortune, he told us about earlier than planned. Already a dyed-in-the-veins, navy-blue Yankees fan, I was ecstatic to learn he had planned an excursion to Ft. Lauderdale to see the Yanks work out during the exhibition season.

A few days after our arrival in Miami, we trekked to the stadium. I was immediately mesmerized by the ease with which we could access players as they went about their morning routines around the park. Tommy John, a big-time pitcher of the era (whom the Yankees had recently acquired from the rival Dodgers) was about to begin a jog. We asked him for an autograph, and were met with a gentlemanly response. He told us he needed "to get [his] run in," but he would be right back at that spot thirty minutes later. Sure enough, he circled back exactly as promised, and pleasantly honored his commitment.

A few more autographs later, we entered the stands to watch the Yankees conduct an informal workout. As it was in 1979, we were able to walk right down and perch above the dugout, leaning over the top of it to catch glances of our admired Pin-Stripers each time the roaming policeman inside the dugout strolled toward the far end. It was almost comical: the cop walked a few paces away, then we leaned over. When he started to pace back in our direction, we would retreat back into our seats. Yes, it was a more innocent time, for sure. He played a token game of cat and mouse: he never intended to clear us out, but he had to appear to be "doing his job."

Eventually, Carmela spotted Ron Guidry in the dugout. Guidry had completed one of the most accomplished pitching campaigns in baseball history the year before. His single season statistics still rank among the best ever. So the idea of a Guidry autograph was so exciting that I couldn't even bear to ask for it myself, fearing he might not consent, and I would be devastated at such a rejection. After all, "Louisiana Lightning," or "The Gator," was not only a phenomenal pitcher, he was a fan favorite for his cool persona and no-nonsense approach to the game. I was really glad that Carmela was feeling less timid than I, and I could only dare to hope that she would be successful when she asked for his signature.

She beckoned him a few times, calling out for his autograph. My anxiety grew with each unmet request; I feared the cop on the beat eventually would direct her away from the dugout. I guess being an attractive and charming twenty-two-year-old didn't hurt her chances of success, but I imagine it was more the tone in her voice as she varied the contents of her plea on her final attempt.

"Come on, Ron... have a heart!" she sang out with an increased volume and noticeably heightened pitch of desperation. And, like coming to the kitchen after Ma called for dinner, up came Guidry's illustrious southpaw to grab the paper and pen from Carmela's outstretched arm and fully extended heart. That was the day that Ron Guidry gave us all a gift, a confirmation of sorts to this eleven-year-old Yankee fan with a bulky cast on his broken right arm. It was true: I learned that day that sometimes even the biggest of stars do have hearts, and my heart was lifted forever on that surreal, sunny Florida day.

As magical and thrilling as that glorious day was, I never imagined faith, fate, and another heartfelt plea to The Gator would bring about a second exhilarating moment for the DiCristos twenty-seven years later. Both Victoria and Nora (then thirteen and twelve) were raised with huge doses of Yankee culture beginning at age zero, and they enjoyed the opportunity to attend a game now and then. We lived in Florida at the time, so when the Yanks played the Rays in St. Petersburg, we could watch them.

While Nora enjoyed the Yankees some, especially going to games, Victoria was deeply magnetized by Yankee lore and tradition as soon as she could grasp even the basics of what it meant to be a Yankee. She learned early on why there would never be another slugger like Ruth or class act like Joe D. She knew why Lou was such a special person, that simply honoring him with the title of "Lou" was the best way to do him justice. She understood how certain Yankees continued upholding the time-honored traditions of those former greats, like Munson, Guidry, and Mattingly. I taught her a lot about the important role the Yankees played in my childhood, and how one year—a most magical 1978—a dozen miracles happened on the field. Ron Guidry was an integral part of many of them. The walls of Victoria's room were donned in home navy and road gray, and hanging on one of those walls was a Burger King poster of the '78 Yanks (a game-day promotion from that year). It was tattered, and not quite flat after being rolled up in a storage box for nearly thirty years. I often reflected on how Guidry started the year off with thirteen wins and no losses, and how he wound up at twenty-five wins against only three losses. Nine of those games were shutouts and sixteen complete games. And most importantly, he got his twenty-fifth win on a windy day in Boston after *we* and the dreaded team from New England needed an extra one-game playoff to decide who would move on to the postseason. Not to mention, he closed out the rival Royals swiftly, and then won the pivotal third game against the Dodgers, after the Yanks dropped the first two contests, leading to a World Series win. All of this glorious energy was further amplified when we watched Guidry, now in his fifties, serve as the pitching coach on the then-current Yankee team.

So the stage was perfectly set when we planned on seeing the Yanks play the Rays in St. Petersburg, Florida, for a couple games of a weekend series. We stayed at the Vinoy hotel after learning the Yanks lodged there. If the stars aligned properly, fans sometimes could get firsthand access to some of the players. After the Friday evening game, we returned to the Vinoy and joined about fifty other fans in the front of the hotel, hoping to see some Yankees return from the game. The big-time stars were usually whisked in via private entrances away from the hoopla; but some others, we were told, would likely come our way. And, if they consented, they might sign some autographs.

Our initial prospects didn't look too bright. A few players went by without stopping to engage anyone. In fact, one notable star even turned away a young boy who had excitedly and unintentionally crossed a rope barrier with a ball and pen seeking a signature. He was so enthusiastic that he even dropped his ball. My daughters and I were disappointed at the arrogance of this player, who remained disinterested as the child was shuffled back to his parents. We remained hopeful, nonetheless. Then, a car pulled up and out came two Yankee coaches who were unrecognized by the novice fans. Tony Peña, the bench coach, and Ron Guidry himself began to matter-of-factly stroll past us and make their way into the hotel. Nearly paralyzed in a state of surprise and awe, I blurted out as Ron, who was following Tony, passed us.

"Hey, Ron," I said, "quick autograph for my daughters?"

What followed was the shortest emotional roller-coaster I can recall. At first, choosing to ignore me and continue walking, The Gator kept his pace, uttered nothing, and went past me and my daughters who stood behind me. Over the next one-and-a-half seconds, which seemed like an hour, my heart dropped to my feet. I simultaneously felt disbelief, sadness, and gargantuan disappointment for my girls, who had immediately joined me in my childlike enthusiasm upon seeing Guidry in person. I dreaded the instantly apparent prospect of having to explain to my innocent kids why Louisiana Lightning blew by us like one his high heaters of yesteryear. I would have to make sense of that baffling maneuver myself. And then, with the same low-key coolness and incredible effectiveness that defined The Gator for more than a decade on the hill, without breaking stride, he murmured just loud enough for me to hear, "Follow me inside."

I never even turned back to tell my kids to follow me. I didn't want to risk alerting and potentially attracting those scores of faux fans to the fact that we had been summoned inside by Yankee royalty.

As we filed in the hotel, like goslings after imprinting on their mother goose, Ron directed us toward the elevator so that he could take a moment without creating additional fanfare. We were all ecstatic to have been given this private opportunity.

"Ron, will you sign my hat?" Victoria requested, not even thinking to remove it from her head. I snapped a photo as Victoria's hat and Nora's notebook were, to their immeasurable delight, "christened." Awestruck and happiful beyond even what my daughters were feeling in this serendipitous melding of Yankee lore and the present, I proudly told Ron, "I got you in spring training in '79 and here again in '06—Thanks!"

I remain forever grateful to Ron Guidry for taking the time to make three kids' nights (one who happened to be thirty-eight). In doing so, he kept the dream alive in all of us. It was only a minute's time, but it was long enough to bolster the faith within our hearts in the goodness of people. Not everyone famous becomes too large for life; sometimes a man's kids get a chance to experience—firsthand—some of the magic of his childhood while he gets to relive it.

How Old Are You Now?

A Birthday Truth

My parents started me in kindergarten early—at the age of four and a half. They thought doing so was prudent, since I was smart enough. The consideration of the potential negative, emotional consequences of starting early was not on the societal radar, nor on my parents'. My family didn't do pre-K (if it even existed yet) or any other forms of nursery school, which is what I remember early schooling being called then. Enrolling me young wasn't allowed, since my fifth birthday wasn't until February, far past the cut-off point. My mom reminded me that (if anyone asked) I was to tell them I was *five,* not four. I didn't think too much about my fibbing duty as I practiced ABCs and showed off my budding acumen for numbers during the first few months. I was initially, happily preoccupied enough with the jet-black hair, pointy nose, and dark-eyed smile of Marilyn, who sat in front of me and often turned around to interact. I even told her my real age once, hoping to impress her twofold—that I was smart enough to be in school already and that I was keeping a big secret. She didn't believe me, which prompted me to leave her perception as it was, lest I blow my cover.

However, a few months later, the chronological worlds of truth and fiction inevitably collided, resulting in one of my earliest memories of intense embarrassment. For the full effect of boyhood trauma, it happened on my birthday. As was customary in Public School 26's kindergarten, the class sat in a circle when a student had a birthday so they could sing two songs for the celebrant. "Happy Birthday" went well enough, other than my feeling severely awkward at being the solitary focus of the room for the thirteen seconds of the jingle. Then, all the dozen kids or so followed Mrs. Bevilacqua's direction, keeping perfect key to what felt like an interrogative firing squad set to music.

"How old are you now? How old are you now? How ooooooold are you now-owwwwwwww? How old are you now?" the class sang.

Compelled by the melodic peer pressure of my classmates, I replied almost spontaneously. Honesty took control of my vocal chords.

"Five," I blurted out.

I felt the blood drain out of my youthful soul. My keen perceptual skills noticed the look of surprise on Mrs. Bevilacqua's brow when she asked me for clarification.

"You mean six, don't you, Silvio?"

"Fiiive," I repeated, holding up one outstretched handful of fingers. I elongated the "i" to avoid compounding the months-old lie I had cosmically resented having to maintain. Ironically, I yielded to a stronger, childish impulse to be recognized for my true age. A few seconds afterward, however, my immediate and clumsy liberation felt stifled and sinful. It was replaced by a dreadful feeling of immediate and potent nausea. I realized I had committed a serious act of dereliction to family duty, and that a phone call home was sure to follow from Mrs. Bevilacqua. I had a hunch she still leaned toward my apparent, odd state of confusion as a more likely explanation of events than a family cover-up, although she was wrong.

As often happens with such seemingly irreconcilable tragedies in the eyes of a young child, the adults worked things out one way or another, and my ability to stay in school was uncompromised, despite my family's dishonest complicity. As I entered home that afternoon, all my mom said was, "The school called, and they know how old you are."

My birthday incident—one filled with high anxiety and tangled discord rather than sugary cupcakes and happiful glances from Marilyn—aptly demonstrates how my early start was far more trouble than it was worth. I didn't realize, until forty years or so later, the extent of the negative effects of starting school prematurely, how being "ahead" of my peers wasn't the best place to be. While it was a good feeling to be consistently recognized for high achievement from kindergarten through high school, as the youngest student, I felt more acutely the drawbacks of being a step behind my peers. Emotionally, I struggled to cross certain developmental stages as quickly as they did. Using the boys' room in a crowd, eating lunch, and conversing with peers were all more difficult to master. I was also forced to adopt a late-bloomer approach in the most important arena: interacting with the new and curious female species. Looking back, it wasn't so bad to have that part of my development a bit behind the curve. After all, being able to conjure my innocent, naïve, boyish charm does have its present-day benefits.

Where's the Dog?

A Memorable Trip

I had nothing against being home with my parents during the evening when I was sixteen, but I liked hangin' out at P.S. 48, "The Park," with my friends much more. After negotiating repeated deals with my mom about how many school nights I was permitted to go out during the week, I would inevitably use up my tokens of freedom too quickly. Craving additional time with my peers, I'd persuade my mom to renegotiate our latest understanding. She had no chance at winning this game of teenage tug of war outright, but she would often salvage at least a partial concession from me. This particular fall night in 1984, I placated her by agreeing to walk our dog, Rocky, as I went to kill a couple hours with my friends, thereby attaching something productive to my rendezvous with the crew.

It was an average-size group of seven or eight of my friends there when I arrived with our dog; they stood around one of the dimly lit handball courts at the far end of the playground. A few were smoking cigarettes, others circulated a joint, and the "burnout" of our bunch, Randy, did both while he corralled his signature eight-pack of seven-ounce Budweiser "nips." Most of us had experimented with a handful of drugs by our mid-teens, undergoing the principal rite of passage in the neighborhood. At this point in my juvenile mood-altering career, I smoked cigarettes daily, pot fairly regularly, and drank beer on most weekends. I hadn't yet progressed to bigger and better things. This night, though, Johnny Oso, one of the coolest kids in our circle, arrived to "hang for a few."

Oso was a lanky kid, around six feet tall. He was rarely seen without a lit Marlboro dangling from the side of his mouth like an extra appendage. His strong presence was even more captivating that night as he approached the crowd and offered a collective, "What's up?" claiming his standing position in the widening circle. I sensed he had something to say, and I was right.

"I picked up a sheet of acid; if anyone wants to drop a hit, you can have one for five bucks." It was standard practice to announce when one of us copped some good weed or something special as Oso had. It was like a supermarket announcement from the loudspeaker, keeping shoppers posted on wild salmon markdowns or tri-tip specials. I asked him a couple of questions about what the high would be like. Several of my friends were happy to interject their firsthand experiences. Then, I proceeded to place a tab of LSD on my tongue, as if it were as commonplace as eating a bowl of Corn Pops for a snack before bed.

This was the matter-of-fact way I was introduced to most drugs. It wasn't really peer pressure at work, at least not in the way the phenomenon is often cited as a direct culprit for such illicit behavior. The drugs were simply there; I twisted my own arm.

Around thirty minutes later, I was thinking that either Oso's sheet of acid was blank tabs, which he got "gypped" on, or maybe acid didn't affect me like it did everyone else who had ever ingested it. I wasn't seeing the "trails" when moving my hand in front of my face, or other cool hallucinations that my more experienced friends had assured me I would see. Many of them were eagerly anticipating a vicarious thrill when I was to start "tripping." Billy V. even mentioned that it might not have been the best idea for me to drop a hit when I had to be home soon.

Still unaware of any effects, and realizing Billy was right—I should be getting myself and the dog home shortly—I readied myself to split for the night. My intentions of keeping my curfews were always good; yet for one reason or another, failing to execute those wishes was the norm. Tonight, it seemed like I would at least get credit for one mark on the ledger of my mom's good side.

As I issued my group "layta," and gave the dog a pull on the leash to go, I noticed something interesting in the starlit sky. I had never observed such a peculiar phenomenon, and wondered why no one else had mentioned it. I saw, underneath the plentiful array of bright stars visible that night, that there was an entire second level of stars underneath the regular stars, closer to Earth. The second level of stars was brilliant, with easily more than three times the number of stars than the regular ones above it. Even more impressive was how the underlying net of stars was moving in a circular motion around the world against the fixed backdrop of the normal night's sky, as I now began to excitedly describe it to my friends. I didn't realize what was really happening, even after several minutes of hyperbolic rambling about what I believed to be a previously unwitnessed galactic occurrence. It took the slurred sounds of devilish chuckling by several of my friends for me to realize what they already knew—my first trip had begun.

My newly discovered, twirling astrological wonder was sufficiently captivating my perverted senses; yet there were dozens more, equally mesmerizing, rare events occurring all around me. I felt intense euphoria and riveting intrigue. Everything was friggin' funny. I was incessantly astonished by potent observations of all varieties, which spanned the entire spectrum of meaning. I realized so much that had previously eluded me. Vinny Pips was real short and pretended it didn't bother him to exist at chest level in the world. Gary lied about everything, but no one ever called him on it. Everyone made sounds, even when they didn't. Robert had a uniquely shaped nose, which seemed to separate from his face for a few seconds at a time and then reattach itself. I lit a cigarette. It was already well-lit, but I thought doing so made sense because it needed to be "more lit, just in case." I had a watch on my wrist. Robert's nose was still unique and doing its gnarly, hilarious trick. Fat Tommy was the most fucked-up guy in our crowd, twenty-two years old and dealing pot for a living. Yet I understood for the first time how all of us, to varying degrees, envied his status among the park wannabes. I liked that he had "juice," and I was addicted to the idea of it, especially because getting the girl I wanted to adore me seemed a much more challenging task.

My parents had no idea how many lies my brother Paul and I told them daily, and there was no way to ever share the realities of our secret world with them. I realized I had just chain-smoked the last six cigarettes, but forgot to drag on any of them. Robert's nose! Our circle had a sound of its own, a blend of the normal sounds of talking and a concurrent distortion of talking. I laughed at this funny, faulty perception for minutes. I kept laughing for an unknown block of time at how no one was even saying anything to me while I cracked up for so long. I had a watch on my wrist. I looked at it.

Oh shit, I thought. It was 11:30 already, two hours later than I was expected to be home. That's what Robert and his nose were talking about when they said I might lose my sense of time. I spent the next ten minutes (was it ten?) walking home quickly, counting the cracks in the sidewalk and being sure not to step on any in the process. There was no point in these obsessive behaviors, other than the slight calming I hoped engaging in them might produce in my frantic and anxious mind. I ruminated on what I would say when I walked in, extremely late, to the angry disbelief my mom was sure to express.

What if my father was awake, too? Oh shit! Fuck! Why did I stay out so late again? Despite being an accomplished excuse maker—who could typically produce and deliver the most instantaneous, plausible, nuanced, apologetic tales of bullshit known to humans—I was playing with a short deck this night. The acid had impaired all my senses, cross-wiring them in the process, not to mention how it had also seemed to diminish my motor skills. I could walk home pretty steadily out of habit, but the notions of managing keys, doorknobs, shoes, socks, and, God forbid, articulation, all seemed to require superhuman skills. As I approached home, I wasn't even able to concoct and mentally rehearse a couple of my old reliables, like "ran into a girl and lost track of time," or "I wound up watching a movie at a friend's and fell asleep." Fumbling with my keys, I felt a psychedelic sense of colossal dread.

I managed to get the door open after a few tries, then attempted to step inside the foyer silently. My mom, in what seemed like half a second, broke through the divide between our two worlds, entering mine by switching on the light. I was an escaping convict who, while stammering in the prison yard, was suddenly located, frozen by the watchtower spotlight. I leaned against the wall, attempted to hide my unsteady gait, and pretended to encounter a knot in taking off my sneakers. Hoping desperately my mom would vanish, I never looked up toward her, fearing she would hear my triple dilated pupils or smell my ongoing stream of incessant and bizarre thoughts. Ma spared both of us the twenty questions that would have befitted the scene, choosing instead to keep it simple, asking me plainly and in a monotone voice devoid of its usual enthusiasm,

"Where's the dog?"

The dog? My momentary state of confusion prompted me to finally look up at my mom, who glared long enough in return to refresh my memory of the facts—that we did indeed have such a pet and that I had utterly lost track of it somewhere at the park. My adolescent lying engine clamored reflexively,

"Paul has him," I forced out, referring to my brother who was still out. He had been with me at the park earlier and had a later curfew, so it was conceivably true. He might have grabbed the dog after I completely forgot about it. But when I lied about it then, I had no idea if Paul were even still out or possibly at home watching *Star Trek* in his room. My mom looked at me with exasperation and disgust, sensing that my claim was no more than a cornered cat's defensive hiss.

"He better be with Paul!" she warned sternly with palpable anger, adding, "I don't even wanna know what you took; just get upstairs!"

I spent the next seven hours lying in bed and watching *The Odd Couple, Star Trek, Mary Tyler Moore,* and whatever else came on through the wee hours. I laughed at the reruns I had seen many times prior, which weren't particularly funny, sans LSD. I found the shows comical as well as the television set itself, the odd way the ceiling and walls were coming together that night, fighting each other for the coveted spots on the four corners for hours.

Later, I heard Paul come in with the dog. I should have been relieved, or at least felt something, but I was too high to attach any feeling to something as uninteresting and normal as that, despite the ordeal I had put my mom through. As the night clumsily morphed into dawn, the humorous, pleasurable aspects of everything that contained atoms just hours ago, faded, replaced by a sense of dysphoria, chills, and uneasy tiredness. I remembered how Oso said that "coming down" sucked, and it would take hours. Eventually, I began to feel a welcomed sense of normal tiredness set in. I felt a kind of body hangover that I had not experienced before, but was glad I was about to crash for a much-needed few hours. I began to doze off into what I knew would be a peaceful sleep, my sobering intuition grateful in the knowledge that I was almost back to normal.

I had forgotten something, though, something that my alarm clock rudely and emphatically proclaimed with an insultingly loud, 1980s-era buzz. It was Wednesday, and I had to get up for school. There would be no deals to make with my mom so that I could stay home for the day and recover. She knew that the best medicine to treat me on that now awfully morose morning was an old-fashioned dose of reality. I dreaded, feared, and worried about the prospect of having to go through a normal day—walking, talking, and sitting in class for hours. It all seemed like components of an army boot-camp obstacle course. Regardless, I knew my mom was right. She let me learn the hard way.

The Little Fish and the Big Heart

Water Seeks Its Own Level

My ex-wife's family had a cabin they shared with some friends in the Adirondacks. Most summers, the kids and my ex would spend a few days there. Being raised in Brooklyn with summers at the ocean a hundred miles east, not Upstate like my ex and her family, I preferred to spend as little time as possible among black-fly swarms, the mice-ridden cabin, annual Lyme disease scares (if not actual contractions) and the other hallmarks of a "charming" getaway to The Lake. So, I typically applied my vacation time to other opportunities with my family, leaving them to enjoy this one alone. One year, however, I made an appearance, and it turned out to be entirely worthwhile, based on a serendipitous experience I shared with my daughter Nora.

As a kid, I enjoyed summer fishing out on the east end of Long Island. I had fun with my family, and particularly enjoyed the excitement and mystery of whether anything would bite on a given day. My brother Paul and I would often walk down to the local marina in Noyack and fish off the dock for snappers. Strolling through the neighborhood (as young as seven and six) we carried poles with bobbers, buckets, bait, a tackle box, and a boatload of enthusiasm. We made pretty good Norman Rockwell subjects, I imagine. So, even though I felt like an awkward city slicker in the middle of the woods of Upstate New York, I was pleased to grab a couple of poles for some fishing off the dock with Nora. Fishing was something (despite the otherwise uncomfortable environs) I knew I enjoyed.

It was a beautiful morning and there was an atypical break in the usual barrage of visiting insects, who loved our hair, face, nose, and whatever else they could bite. This welcomed respite from the bugs didn't last more than a few hours, of course, but it did make for a nice time for Nora (then eight) and me to enjoy the sun and catching a few freshwater trout. We threw them all back, since they were small and we weren't really fishing for dinner.

Nora reeled in a pretty small trout, so we proceeded to execute our recently devised assembly line process to remove the hook from its mouth and toss him back quickly. This consisted of Nora holding her pole while I put mine down to grab her line and handle the slimy task of unhooking and returning the little guy to his lake. When I grabbed her fish with one hand and began to carefully attempt to undo the hook, I saw that it was caught and twisted in the fish's mouth pretty firmly. Nora and I winced and cringed in unison as I tugged and twisted, with increasing desperation, trying unsuccessfully to free the hook from its mouth to toss it back. With each unwitting bruise I inflicted upon the helpless, entangled trout, it felt as if both of our hearts were also being struck.

Our moods darkened as quickly as the life visibly drained out of this poor, little, mangled fish on the hook. Time was running out, as this was all being done above the dock. I couldn't help splitting my focus momentarily between the urgent task at hand and the sad look of terror and emerging resignation on Nora's face. Her head pointing down, lips pursed and eyes now softened with grief, I could sense that she was troubled, not only by the fish's life fading into the open air but by my visibly growing angst in trying to save it and spare them both further pain. Before we knew it, it was too late. As I finally separated this would-be throwback from the instrument of its demise, dropping it guiltily back into its former home, Nora and I peered down into the water, now a glimmering cemetery, still hoping for the impossible.

At the time, I felt sad about killing the fish, unable to shield Nora from seeing it die in such a frustrating episode. Of course, I knew it wasn't a colossal issue. We would probably not think too much about it in a few minutes time. I would move on to angrily swatting away black flies and trying to decide whether to wash myself in the "shower" my in-laws had built (very little water pressure and even less privacy), and Nora would happily search for forest gnomes in the woods with her sister Victoria. On another level, though, perhaps one a father intuits, something bigger and more profound was happening within my daughter's soul as well as my own; I felt affected by this well below the surface.

As we would continue to experience and understand many times in the years to come, Nora and I share a keen and finely tuned emotional radar of the world and each other. Our sense of openness and vulnerability has anchored our characters in beautiful, fundamental ways while also leaving us easy targets for the daily harshness presented by the Universe (or by a small lake in the

Adirondacks). So it's hard, balancing the need to live life while managing complex, emotional hyper-awareness, certainly in a world where you can't act on those emotions all the time. This is true for both of us. Part of our success in this journey has been learning to avoid certain vulnerable emotional circumstances altogether. One lesson we learned for certain: neither of us has ever fished again.

Victoria Visits the YanYans

Life at a Higher Frequency

"Well, obviously a whole bunch of them kind of just gather together in the air at Yankees games," Victoria said to me in the familiar, authoritative tone she started using around age three.

"Even when they're losing?" amused, I asked my then-seven-year-old daughter.

"Yeah, Dad," she answered, as if stating the obvious, "at home games. Because even if they're losing, the power of the Yankees at the stadium attracts the YanYans."

"The YanYans also float above babies," I told her, constructing more parameters for our new imaginary creatures.

"Yeah!" Victoria replied. "Because babies always look like they're staring at things we can't see. But only *certain* babies."

"Did you know that certain people also can see them?" I said.

"Really?" she asked, seeming to forget that we had created the YanYans only minutes before.

"Oh, sure. It's been documented,"

"Have *you* seen them?"

"Only once. And it was very special," I looked at her fallen face and realized that she was probably wondering why she hadn't seen them yet. "You know, though, people aren't really supposed to see them. But certain people, people like us, even if we can't see them with our eyes like babies can, can feel them when they're around."

It worked. Perking up, she exclaimed, "Like right now! I feel them!"

"Me too," I said, smiling. And in a way, I did.

Seated on my couch around noon, laptop placed as usual, a business call occupied my right ear and most of my attention via a cordless phone propped up by my extended shoulder to the side of my head. It was 2003, and I had been working from home for the last year or so in the new, lucrative world of digital advertising. Things were going well financially, the kids were thriving in elementary school, and there wasn't much to complain about.

While attempting to pay earnest attention to the maniacal ramblings of one of those hyper-entrepreneurial types, who was still early into his phone pitch—going on about how, soon enough, smartphones "will automatically furnish us with coupons for pizza, movie admissions, and hotel stays based on our physical location at any given moment," the house phone rang in the kitchen. I rarely answered it during business hours, so I let the answering machine do its thing.

A few moments later, alerted by what sounded like a short, frantic message from my then-wife, Kathy—only partially audible against the drone of the Steve Jobs wannabe—I dropped the phone and checked the message. She was crying, horrified, and in a frenzy. She was doing her best to quickly explain the situation so she could leave work immediately. The school had called her and explained that our older daughter Victoria, age ten at the time, had undergone some kind of medical incident during choir practice. I called them immediately, and they informed me that Victoria suddenly "froze" and "became completely rigid while remaining standing." The only visible movement was "her eyes blinking repeatedly," and she showed "no signs of consciousness."

After the choir director attempted to talk to her and got no response, a phys-ed instructor, who was apparently in great physical condition, grabbed Victoria from under her arms and carried her down the hall to the nurse's office, like moving a bronze statue. She remained stiff and unresponsive, so he placed her on the examination table while the nurse and others tried to determine what happened. She had a good pulse and was breathing, although she had turned somewhat blue momentarily, and was still utterly non-responsive for almost ten minutes. They called Kathy immediately after Victoria began to snap out of it, explaining that she had "some kind of spell," was still foggy, and that an ambulance was on the way. We could either go to the school or meet them directly at the emergency room.

I had recently bought a three-year-old, red Acura, and had it for a trial period. Living about two miles from the school, I decided to race there, rather than have Victoria transported alone in the ambulance somewhere twenty-plus minutes away. This wasn't the test drive I had in mind. My red blur zoomed out of my driveway. Fearing I might get pulled over for speeding, which would cause a tragic delay, I took my chances anyway, flooring it through the rural, winding Hudson Valley roads. I parked in the first spot I saw at the school, slammed the door behind me, and streaked across the front lawn. I could feel the stares of children and adults in and out of the school building taking notice of the urgency and speed of my frenzy.

As I arrived, Victoria was answering questions about how she felt and what she remembered of what took place. She reported "going blank" in choir and recalled nothing until she awoke on the table a minute or so before I arrived. Though still in a stupor, she also had an apparent sense of well-being. No one present in the nurse's office quite understood what happened. She didn't faint; she remained standing, but she was totally unaware of what had transpired. All I could do was attempt to comfort her by explaining that we were leaving to get her checked out at the hospital. I assured her that I would ride with her and that the ambulance was just a necessary precaution.

Truthfully, I was as scared as she was, maybe more so, as the biological aftermath of her incident seemed to have left her in a relatively calm state of mind. With my best poker face on, we hopped into the ambulance. At one point, Victoria asked if she had fainted, and I said she had, figuring that would be a satisfactory explanation to allay her concern and not having a better answer at the moment. The ambulance driver tactlessly contradicted me, adding that "if she fainted, she would have displayed X and Y behavior," but "this was definitely something else." If he weren't responsible for driving us, I would have broken knuckles on his teeth simply because his emotional idiocy was anything but comforting to my already-traumatized daughter. Thankfully, we arrived at Goshen Hospital and were rid of his infuriating lack of empathy.

Victoria's mother arrived via her own frantic drive from work. Victoria was now in a bed in a section of the emergency room, her vitals being checked and other tests scheduled. She complained of an increasing headache, and true to her form, she asked for food. *That's one positive sign*, I thought. Over the next few hours, doctors and nurses poked, prodded, needled, CT-scanned, MRI'd, and X-Ray'd Victoria as a neurologist sought to zero in on a diagnosis. They informed us that she had a seizure, and while this was potentially serious and would need further exploration, they found no other underlying medical problem that could have plausibly caused a sudden seizure. This was a small consolation to us. We were advised that a pretty high minority of teenagers have a seizure at least once, and that a single incident didn't necessarily signal an ongoing condition. We were also referred to a child neurologist, whom we planned to see the next day.

The doctor was a wonderful woman with a great bedside manner and obvious mastery of her craft. She armed us with the facts, which, at that juncture, were straightforward and anything but comforting. The bright side was that there was no evidence of any underlying problems that caused the seizure. However, the scary truth was that ruling out an epilepsy diagnosis at this stage was impossible. The only viable medical approach at this point was to wait and see if Victoria had another seizure. If she were to have another, medication would almost certainly be advised. Our high anxiety was matched by our hopefulness as we prepared to wait.

Two weeks later, one afternoon, I stepped out of the kids' playroom, which doubled as my home office, to see what Kathy was cooking. Victoria was playing a computer game at a desk adjacent to mine. When I came back a minute or so later, she was on the floor, flat on her back, convulsing violently from head to toe. I dropped to my knees beside her in microseconds, directed by a surge of parental instincts. I turned her on her side and made sure she was clear of any stray toys and furniture. Victoria's younger sister Nora sensed the quick commotion, left her room, and stood in the doorway. She was immediately horrified, seeing Victoria as she was, and looked right through me. In a high-pitched and hurried voice, she asked, "Why is Victoria doing that?"

The confusion and terror widened her already large, almond-shaped eyes. She dropped her lower lip in fearful disbelief. Hers was a look I immediately knew I would always remember.

"Victoria will be OK soon, Pal," I said. "The doctor told us this might happen. Please, go get Mom. Quick."

Kathy mirrored Nora's shock as she entered the room, but she quickly composed herself. I continued kneeling next to Victoria and began saying things to her that I intuited might be calming—in case she could actually hear me on some level. I assured her it was OK, that she must have wanted to go into her own world and imagine eating macaroni by herself, that we knew she would be back soon. As her convulsing stopped after an eternal minute or so and she lay on the floor motionless, Kathy reminded me that we didn't need to do anything, as long as she was breathing. She would come out of it shortly. I continued with my fantastic utterances in a wishful, desperate effort to comfort Victoria and ourselves, telling her she "must have been visiting some YanYans in their special world." Victoria regained consciousness. She was disoriented and feeling a brief sense of euphoria, but we explained to her what occurred.

These are common phenomena for someone after experiencing a tonic-clonic seizure. A thousand facts like these would soon become part of our family's vocabulary, as Victoria's diagnosis of juvenile myoclonic epilepsy was later confirmed by her neurologist.

There was a lot to learn. We began to face what became a defining challenge in Victoria's life. The same kind of fear and dreadful uncertainty defining that terrifying incident became a palpable, daily sensation we learned to live with: the mystery and unpredictability of epilepsy.

I also felt another feeling that day, one with even greater magnitude than the angst and worry. I felt a deeper love for my daughter than I had ever experienced for anything. Witnessing the first person I had ever truly, unconditionally loved in such a state of complete vulnerability gripped me. It changed me. It etched an even deeper chamber into my heart from which to love her and everything else in the world, I later discovered. Of course, I would have given anything I could have to trade places with Victoria that day, sparing her of such a difficult and serious neurological condition. I still would. But I remain grateful for the silver lining, for the awareness I gained. I took some solace in knowing that whenever Victoria's body compelled her to visit the YanYans again, I could go with her—at least in spirit.

More than 5,000 days have passed since those frightful moments riveted us, humbling our hearts and minds to the truth of the human body's unjust imperfections. For me, those fifteen years have come with feelings of personal angst, worry, and sometimes outright horror at what epilepsy has made me witness. Or even worse, to hear about seizures from afar, unable to help, sitting on my white-leather couch in California, trying to sound brave despite my own tumult, asking, "How ya feelin', Pal?" as I console my daughter over the phone, post-spell. These years have also brought me a textbook familiarity with neurological terms and symptoms: tonic-clonic, absence seizure, postictal, aura.

The grander narrative, though, is one that belies Victoria's petite stature. It demonstrates how one need not be defined by their limitations but can instead use them as a springboard for uber-resilience and gargantuan accomplishment. Epilepsy, "the dirty word" and diagnosis assigned to my daughter, has transformed into so much more than a name or an illness.

When she entered high school, I didn't reflect on her multiple tonic-clonic seizures and five medication changes. Instead, I bragged to anyone who would listen to the story of how "she decided to go on a student exchange to Ecuador" in her junior year. And, how when denied permission from her principal, she politely congratulated him, "Thank you so much for pioneering the first exchange program at Cherokee High School, Mr. Dang." I equate her experience at Cherokee High with determination, resilience, and proficiency. Never epilepsy.

I remained humbled and impressed in her college years when she completed two majors and a concentration (while working full-time, graduating with a completed thesis, honors, and admission into three honors societies). Epilepsy is only a small part of her collegiate story. When the director kicked her out of a choir for "unexcused absences," or after having a spell during work that required three sets of stitches on her face and two repaired teeth, or even when she underwent minor surgery in the middle of her final exams, Victoria was undeterred. Epilepsy never defined her experience. She came out with more friends, more empathy, and more determination than I've ever witnessed. College for Victoria was growth, hard work, and willpower. Not epilepsy.

She has helped me understand true and honest feminism, and I still delight in telling colleagues and friends the story of how, with principled logic and Socratic ease, she refused to change her capstone presentation on sex education in schools simply because her myopic and rude education department chair—in his frustrated attempts to push his misogynistic paradigm—disagreed with her stance against abstinence-only education. There she earned her only B in her education classes—not for lack of knowledge or research, but for commitment to principles and her own ideals. That she later endured a tonic-clonic seizure in his office while protesting his unfair grading is not the highlight of this story. Nor did she let it stop her from fighting his close-minded anachronistic views. Her persistence, righteousness, and feminism defined Victoria's fight. Not epilepsy.

After college, Victoria continued to make meaningful impacts on the lives of others while effecting change from inside institutions in desperate need of revision. Spending the next three years teaching Spanish (and life) in two different boarding schools and refusing to listen to anyone who told her to "take it easy" or "give it time," Victoria broke antiquated, ill-informed rules and impacted the lives of many students, as both schools quickly learned that they hired someone who gave more than they bargained for. She continued her relentless approach of placing principles before personalities and unjustified hierarchy. The multiple seizures she had in her class only helped her students model the same empathy she preached to them every day. Role model, empath, and educator define Victoria's career as a teacher. Not epilepsy.

And now, she begins her next adventure: a Ph.D. in Hispanic Literature and Advanced Feminist Studies (which she heard about offhand while modeling for an art class, and applied an hour before the application was due). A week after her submission, the joint heads of the program called her for an interview conducted in Spanish. When the interview was over, they asked her to clarify where she was from. She mentioned, somewhat cautiously, so she would not sound corrective (since she had mentioned it moments ago) that she was from New York. Based on her fluency, they were astonished that she was not a native Spanish speaker, and presumed she must have been born in Latin America. How's that for being "disabled?"

Victoria has been unafraid and pleased to embrace many rich, traditional aspects of her upbringing, including a deep and fervent spiritual practice in her life, a reverence for marriage (despite seeing her parents' union dissolve) and a willingness to tie the knot at a young age by today's standards. Likewise, she has a hands-on approach to caring for the old and sick, and continues to break new ground daily as a young, outspoken, progressive woman.

As I reflect on this dramatic and beautiful journey of hers, and the place epilepsy has occupied in it, I realize that maybe the YanYans we created together really do exist. That even though these imaginary white creatures may not "gather in the air" above us as we'd imagined in her childhood, they dwell, happifully, in my daughter's heart, essence, and spirit, and gratefully, also in mine.

Eve

Bells of Truth

I knew somewhere in my anxious heart in the moments before my wedding ceremony that something was wrong. Sitting alone in a church vestibule minutes before the formal ritual was to commence, I followed Father Joseph's direction to engage in a few minutes of final mental and spiritual reflection about what was about to happen. I wished to be earnest with myself in those last minutes of soul searching, yet the internal storm of ominous, colliding realizations was too worrisome and frightening to face squarely. So, as the dozens of family and friends filled the pews inside the stained-glass confines of Saint Vincent's on a brilliant, summer day in 1991, only so much light would reach my twenty-three-year-old psyche. I chose instead to rationalize away the heart-racing truth of our ill-fated marriage before it was even finalized.

"You know, it's not that bad, Sil," Kathy, my then-wife, said to me while sitting on the edge of our California king bed as I packed my leather duffel bag.

I sighed. The thing is, she was right. It was not that bad.

That spring in 2009, I was forty-one years old and had been married for more than seventeen years. I'm quite certain most men would have been happy, or at least comfortable enough, to stay put. I was earning around $300,000 a year in an economically modest area of Lake Mary, Florida, in a beautiful house in a pretty area of town, sitting on positive equity. I worked five minutes from home as the number-two man in an internet advertising company of about fifty employees, most of whom reported to me. Likewise, my two daughters were doing well in high school.

While Kathy and I had our history of problems and significant difficulties, these conflicts certainly didn't result in us sleeping on opposite ends of our Tempur-Pedic—as many couples do in a rocky marriage. She cooked, took care of the house, and worked full time. And, to top it off, four years earlier, we had each "confessed our sins" one evening in a brutal, refreshingly candid attempt to finally clear the air and put our best feet forward in our marriage. We were all in. We put our cards on the table. Insert your own metaphor here.

Ultimately, we failed. In light of where we stood economically and given the honest efforts we each made over the years, I understood quite well why my wife made that puzzled remark, "It's not that bad." I can't remember if I said anything aloud at that moment, but I do remember thinking clearly: *I want to have more than "not that bad" with someone.* I yearned for something deeper, more compatible, less forced, less compromised, and more organic. I wanted an earnest love, as I admittedly and sadly never had with Kathy.

I finally allowed myself to acknowledge how our getting married so young—a condition I used to scoff at as too simplistic when others offered it as a general explanation of marital failure—was, in fact, a big factor in the demise of our marriage. I accepted what I believe is the kernel of weakness in many bad or failed marriages: we had come together out of mostly need rather than want, and we lacked the ultimate compatibility to survive. I am certain some couples can and do overcome an overly needy beginning versus one based on a more healthy choice in a partner. They may be more compatible or perhaps work harder at it, but what I suspect is true (more often than many would care to admit) is that they remain together in silos of mental, emotional, and spiritual isolation. Anyway, call it a midlife crisis. Label me another schmuck leaving his family when he started to feel "the itch." Regardless, divorce fucking hurts.

I came to realize that I rolled into our marriage on at least three broken wheels, and I was unequipped to give her or myself what we needed emotionally. I was still stricken by grief when we met and soon after married. My father had died at the early age of fifty-eight—three years prior to our wedding—and my thirty-one-year-old brother was killed, suddenly, less than a year after my father. More salt in the wounds came in the form of my first, massive romantic heartbreak shortly after these difficult losses. Truthfully, I didn't realize the deep impact of these events. I hoped that our desire to be married and have kids would trump my hurts.

We blinked a few times, so to speak, and found ourselves with two teen daughters seventeen years later. While there were many times over the years when the bells of truth rang inside me about our incompatibility and lack of true love I needed to feel, I rationalized them into temporary silence. I don't regret doing so. Despite the often-mentioned "wisdom" in splitting for the kids' sake, which asserts that they would be better off away from a conflicted marriage, I was not yet willing to leave my daughters in that way. Whether staying for that long was the right move, I think they can perhaps best answer. At this stage of my life, I was compelled by my truth to open my eyes widely and keep them open. Finally, I admitted the painful truth to myself and my wife.

I screwed up a lot over the years, which, in a nutshell, covered all aspects of the Seven Deadly Sins (or, should you be 12-step inclined, seven defects of character) including finding a young and willing parachute to break the fall of separation shortly before I physically left our home. It was the wrong move, a cowardly one, and remains one of my few honest regrets.

My parachute was a twenty-six-year-old temptress with the biggest blue eyes and the sweetest presence that even Al Pacino's character in *The Devil's Advocate* would have admired for her sinful allure. And I took her bait—hook, line, and ultimately, sinker. She was charming, seductive, flirty, and forward. I was tired, frustrated, and felt guilty for wanting out of my marriage. I was also exhausted from remaining at a job with a maniacal boss, who had become increasingly intolerable. I felt somewhat unwanted and older as a man, and unwilling to continue fighting for my marriage. I was ready to escape.

On the other hand, it wasn't simply a matter of taking a bite out of the twenty-six-year- old apple and yielding to a lustful impulse. It's rarely that simple. My connecting with Eve was also a product of feeling a lack of joy in my life, feeling that I was taken for granted in many ways at home, and a profound sadness and intuitive realization that Eve represented more than just greener grass on the other side. Deep down, although I should have left before I leapt, I better appreciate now how the intense yearning I felt was based largely on having a desperately unfulfilled heart and soul—a condition that no amount of comfort in my home cocoon would have ever remedied. I was desperate, alone, and envious of the few privileged couples who possessed a "one + one = infinity" type of connection, a natural kind of love and commitment that's visible even to the blind and awe inspiring. Somewhere beneath the guilt of wanting out—which I knew would devastate my wife and daughters—and the shame of making what was, in some ways, the biggest mistake one can make in life in choosing the wrong partner, I also felt deserving of a better, more legitimate life with a suitable and proper mate.

I haven't yet found the deep and earnest love I've been searching for in a partner, and that's not the point. I am seeking my truth. Because of this, my unconditional love for my daughters has continued to blossom wonderfully, enveloping my heart. I am free and able to contribute to and engage with the world honestly and unwaveringly.

That's All!

A Perfect Day

There have been several moments when I feel words will never quite do justice to the depth or breadth of my feelings. Sometimes, it feels like I'm painting a Rembrandt with crayons. But I've come to accept this when it comes to expressing the beauty, richness, and spiritual nature of life's most meaningful experiences. One of these magical times, a whole day of sacred times, was May 14, 2016, when my first daughter, Victoria DiCristo, married Langdon James.

Victoria was always a special girl; her vivaciousness and tirelessly optimistic spirit was evident from her first days on the planet. Sleeping through the night seemed to bore her, and she interacted with her mother or me in an endless game of "What will you try next to get me to sleep?" Walking her around, singing, playing music, the baby swing, the rhythms of the washer, dryer, and vacuum, the pleading, praying, and desperate attempts at reasoning that tired parents resort to were all trumped soundly by Victoria's will to sleep only when she was ready.

The arrival of Nora, her younger sister, thirteen months after Victoria, seemed only to embolden Victoria's early, independent spirit, and propensity to direct others. Among Victoria's first verbal phrases was an emphatic "*Stop* looking at me!" if anyone dared to commit such an infraction too early in the morning. "Carry you me!" she'd yell when she was tired of walking on her own. Now, I should point out that neither her mother nor I were softies. We were firm parents who didn't yield reflexively to the myriad demands of our toddlers. And I also don't mean to imply that Victoria was especially difficult to handle. As I suppose it is with a born leader, destined to change the world from the start, Victoria simply made her assertive presence known.

At age three, she declared her intent to become a teacher when she grew up. By age five or six, she was already refining her craft daily with her "classroom" of stuffed animals, whom she positioned appropriately in her room for "school." I imagine that all those *Little House on the Prairie* reruns of Laura, Miss Beetle, and Mary helped spur her passions to teach, and so she did. "Lion! Stay on task! Kitty, good job on your letters! Here's a sticker! Dalmatian, eyes up here, please!"

she asserted from her shared bedroom-turned-classroom.

Victoria also spent much of the next two decades assessing how her teachers could improve their methodologies. At times, she offered them unsolicited suggestions, such as when she decided to prepare her own report cards for each of her second-grade peers, teacher comments included, in order to ensure her actual teacher didn't miss anything.

Her penchant for speaking truth to power, especially educators, remained a cardinal trait throughout her life. Victoria's candor cost her a letter grade in her final year of undergraduate studies, when she reminded a bigoted professor (and department chair) that abstinence was *not* the only true method of birth control. Undeterred, even fueled by such ignorance, Victoria broke in as a feisty, knowledgeable, and, yes, still assertive high school Spanish teacher and immediately connected deeply with her students. She taught from a position of truth, humility, and respect, continuing to hone her remarkable ability to amicably disarm those with differing opinions, leaving them standing on common ground before they knew it.

Victoria's keen powers of assessment and penchant for candor were not limited to the classroom. When she was only five and following me around one morning as I got ready for work—having breakfast together, watching me shave—she asked me why "Mommy had slept on the couch" the night before. Attempting to shield Victoria from the earliest and serious tremors that had begun to rattle our marriage, I fibbed to her and explained that "Mommy couldn't sleep too well and didn't want to keep me awake from her moving around all night," With the matter-of-factness and monotone query of a seasoned detective with twenty years on the force, she simply repeated her question, as if to say, "Dad, you can stop the bullshit now." I gave the honest answer upon the second authoritative prompt and explained that her mom and I were in a fight, and she was mad, so she slept on the couch. Gratefully, this mutual candor remained the norm for us.

So when she met Langdon James in the fall of 2014—he, too, an outstanding teacher (of English) in his own right and a devout idealist—it didn't take long for the forces of nature to manifest, or for

Victoria to make sure they did, just in case. When I got an important midday call from Langdon a few months into their second year of teaching, the absence of his typically articulate and measured delivery—his utterances reduced to an uncharacteristic stammering—I was not completely surprised.

"Umm, well, Sil, I . . . I . . . I didn't write a speech or anything, but, well, so, can I, uhh, marry Victoria?"

What followed was likely the longest twenty-five seconds of his life. I replied that I needed to step into a conference room for privacy's sake, and I proceeded to amble about fifty feet to the nearest one. I said a quick, silent, and poignant Serenity Prayer to myself, and asked the heavens for my spontaneous mental truth to remain unfiltered as I delivered it.

"Well, Langdon," I began, in somewhat of a philosophical and steady tone. "Here's what I think: I don't know you too well yet, but if you and Victoria feel a spiritual connection, who am I to stand in its way?" I realized that I was offering him the same advice and "permission" that Victoria had offered me a little more than a year ago when I asked her opinion about proposing to the woman I was seeing. A few months later, Langdon made it official when he proposed and she accepted.

Victoria and I have always been close, so I wouldn't say we became estranged when I divorced her mother. However, my necessary move across the country to California after our split definitely hurt my relationship with both of my daughters. Coupled with the fact that the few years that followed the divorce were some of the most difficult ones for each of us for a variety of reasons, it's safe to say that we became more distant from each other than ever before. We still visited each other when we could—about once a year in each direction, as she was at Roanoke College in Virginia and I in Southern California. And we never missed the opportunity to give each other earnest best wishes on all the holidays, birthdays, etc. We did our best to stay connected out of a deep love we shared for each other, but a certain bond was surely lacking for a while.

Fortunately, this period did not last, and we started to steadily reestablish the depth and closeness of our relationship as Victoria finished her final two years of college. Cleaning out her dorm room on graduation weekend in 2014, I offered formal amends to her.

"Hey, pal. I wanted to tell you directly that I know Mom and I splitting, and me being across the country the last few years, have not been easy for you at all, and I am really sorry for not being there physically and, more so, emotionally. I'm glad that our relationship has gotten so much better lately and I'm gonna keep doing my best to keep things going in this great direction."

"I know, Dad. Thanks. And I really like the way things are going now." Victoria mirrored my warm sentiments, with a back-and-forth pointing of her index finger signaling her unspoken emphasis on the *between us* aspect of her response. Hearing my choked-up tone and seeing that my eyes had begun to mist, like Charles Ingalls having one of his sappy moments of over-the-top gratitude, she added a playful admonition, "You're not gonna cry now, though. Right?"

We laughed our way out of the slightly awkward healing and overdue exchange, getting back to separating her keeps from her throwaways. Victoria understood where my heart was, and that was all that mattered to me. We've never looked back since.

A few months after Langdon's proposal, I asked Victoria if she had given any thought to the actual wedding—location, potential venues, cost, how I could help, etc. What followed was the most adorable of replies, which reflected the beautiful naiveté of true love and an equally refreshing lack of preoccupation with things material; both qualities epitomized Victoria and Langdon's state of being at the time.

"I was thinking we would just have the wedding at Gigi's house." (Gigi was her great grandmother who died a few years prior and left the annual gathering place for summers at Cape Cod to the family.) "Langdon and I are starting to save money, which I think should be enough by the time we are ready. I also planned to ask you what you could do to help financially, if anything, 'cause I know things have been tough for you. But Langdon and I plan to pull it off either way."

Fortunately, I was finally in a position—despite a challenging alimony responsibility and some recent difficult years in my industry—to help.

"OK, sounds good!" I excitedly replied. "I know I can help to some extent, so why don't we just start exploring some options and see where we stand as we gather information?"

What followed was perhaps the most magical string of events in my life to date, culminating in a wedding that transformed my life forever. Week after week, Victoria and I explored the possibilities for her ceremony. Where, when, properties to rent, food, DJ's, how many guests to invite, and a gazillion other details one never seems to consider until actually embarking on such a task. And, with each passing week, we realized the cost would be higher than anticipated. Thankfully, though, my business was going well, and I was able to keep raising my hand to foot the bills. I was so truly happy to do so. My glee was paralleled by Victoria's exponentially growing excitement about her big day.

Beyond the planning itself, something else precious and beautiful was occurring between us. Victoria got a chance to see how excited I was to have taken on the job as principal wedding planner. I spent many early mornings calling potential caterers, DJ's, and the like on The Cape, and I was only too happy to put all of my business and people-reading skills to work in sifting through who would be best to help us create a phenomenal wedding. It was never about anything grand or over the top for Victoria. If it were possible, she would have humbly preferred using her iPhone with speakers for music and having a few relatives cook for everyone at Gigi's house, two ideas she actually put forth originally. It was only the scale of the event and her desire to enable friends and family to affordably sleep under one roof that necessitated a bigger, more elaborate venue and the enlistment of service professionals to make it happen.

Nonetheless, Victoria's imprint remained indelible at the core of the event. The outdoor venue was at a charming, nine-bedroom Cape Cod home once frequented by such writers as F. Scott Fitzgerald. Her young cousins sang "Here Comes Our Teacher," an honorary song they sang to Victoria each summer when playing "school." After she scarfed down a slice of pre-wedding pizza, I walked her barefoot down the grassy aisle. The numerous toasts, tributes of prose, music, and song offered by so many. Their wedding was as humble, authentic, and beautiful as my daughter. As I delivered my musical salutation of Frank Sinatra's "That's All" to the new Mrs. and Mr. DiCristo, I felt my brother "G," my Dad, and Ol' Blue Eyes himself make a watchful toast from their shared balcony above, straight to my grateful imagination.

What a perfect day it was. I'm not really one of those people who believes everything happens for a reason. But, among the perfect weather, flower crowns, Cape Cod lobster, and musical serenades, I admit I wondered if perhaps this day did.

A Wish

Kelly Patino

My brother Paul is eighteen months older than I, and that margin made a world of difference when I was twelve and he was nearing fourteen. I remember distinctly the day he let me join him in "hangin' out" with his recently acquired friends (girls included) in our Staten Island neighborhood of Dongan Hills. Being granted such coveted access was a thrilling opportunity, almost as fantastic as the idea of going out for pizza with the Yankees.

"Wanna come to church with us tomorrow and hang out after?" Paul matter-of-factly asked me on Saturday night, April 19, 1980.

"Sure! What time we leaving?" I replied, without skipping a beat, my overeagerness threatening to cause him to reconsider the random invitation he'd extended.

"We'll leave at 8:00 and meet everyone at 'The Wall' and walk from there," he said. I was elated. I didn't know who "everyone" was, but I knew girls would be included just from the way Paul had been conducting business over the last few weeks, kind of like the cat who ate the canary, when it came to where he was spending his time. I guess he was finally ready to let me in. I knew meeting at The Wall, where the cool kids (and pretty girls) congregated often, was in itself the equivalent of being knighted into Dongan Hills royalty. I accepted the appointment with silent gratitude and fantasized about how crossing through Paul's secret teenage portal would feel. My anticipatory thoughts kept me up late and served as an early alarm clock the next morning.

The code of expected younger-brother behavior needed no explanation from Paul. Like a bird instinctively understands the cue for its mother's feeding or when it's time to jump from the nest to take flight, I understood the need to play things cool and make my best impression, without tainting Paul's established coolness within the prized neighborhood clique.

I wonder now if that bird first taking flight would be as impressed by its view as I was with mine as Paul's elusive and secret friends came into focus as we approached The Wall from down the block. Paul instructed me on who was who.

"That kid smoking is Tommy Restivo. He's sixteen and we call him 'Resty.' His sister Marie is right next to him. She's fifteen, but has been going out with Joey, who owns the pizzeria, for two years. They say they're gonna get married. See those two girls walking down? They're sisters—Cammy and Kelly Patino. Cammy is fourteen and Kelly is twelve. Cammy and I hung out at 'The Plateau' the other night. It was freezing out, but I kept my hands warm," Paul said with a grin.

"Don't say anything, though!" he barked, temporarily breaking his stoic air of coolness, just in case my naiveté prevented me from realizing how out of line revealing such a disclosure would have been.

"So, Kelly's twelve?" I verified, as we came upon The Wall, now within a half of a block, close enough for me to see Kelly's magical form taking shape before me. Her frame was thin, but curvy. She stood straight and confidently as we made eye contact from a good twenty or thirty feet away. I had never been dying of thirst, lost in the desert, or come upon an oasis—like I saw on Saturday morning cartoons—but I suddenly understood that feeling when Kelly's surveying stare remained fixed on "Paul's little brother," as I would soon be introduced.

Her lips were thick and pronounced. They commanded attention. Her eyes were huge and round, yet soft and inviting. Her hair was long, brown, and wavy, just how I liked it. In the ten seconds that we locked eyes, I knew that Kelly was as approachable as she was pretty, as down to earth as she was gorgeous. Before I even had a conscious inkling of the beautiful and torturous adolescent quicksand I was about to step into, my Kelly-fixated trance was jarringly interrupted.

"Yeah, she's twelve," Paul answered, repeating it since I didn't hear him the first time, and then adding, "She's Resty's girlfriend. They've been going out for months."

Paul might as well have poured cold water on my face, startling me out of what seemed like the best dream ever. This wasn't fair! Kelly was my first real crush, and she was suddenly as unavailable as she was delightful, locked up with a sixteen-year-old who smoked and was about to get his driver's license. I resented this kid before I even shook his hand a few moments later.

A couple of other kids joined our posse as we walked a mile or so to Saint Sylvester's for Mass. I barely noticed them or anything else that morning after meeting Kelly and her annoying and far-too-old boyfriend, who was holding her hand almost constantly as we walked.

Why don't you let her breathe already? She's not a dog on a leash! I thought, knowing I would be so much less stifling than *Resty* was with her. *Resty*. What a silly name, too. So unoriginal.

I was a quick study over the next two weeks or so, learning how to best integrate myself into this new batch of cool kids that my brother had gifted me exposure to. I played the comedian at times, a role I was pretty familiar with already as the family mascot and youngest of five kids. I balanced that with the cute-and-smart-kid role. I was the youngest in my seventh-grade class, playing down my intelligence and being ahead of the curve. This worked particularly well with Kelly, to whom I had managed to get pretty close, even if only "as a friend," a limiting status that she dutifully reminded me of just about every time we interacted. I became pretty creative in finding ways to be alone with her without Resty or even the handful of kids who always seemed to congregate like pesky gnats. I left for school a good hour or so early some mornings so I could walk Kelly (and her sister Cammy, a necessary appendage) to their bus stop since they went to a neighboring school. Paul joined a couple of times, but, thankfully, he bailed out soon after in favor of sleep. His interest in Cammy was purely hormonal, not grand and epic like my romantic longings for Kelly. I would also meet Kelly earlier at The Wall before the crew reported for hangin' duty on weekday afternoons and weekends. I became quite familiar with sixteen-year-old Resty's schedule, craftily exploiting the fact that, although his being older gave him obvious advantages, schedule availability was not one of them. I wiggled my way into a close, between-the-lines-enough connection with Kelly to provide me with a steady flow of blissful fascination, which catapulted me into the wonderful, mysterious, and happiful world of girls. Kelly remained partially off-limits since she was going out with Resty, but even this damper wasn't enough to thwart my feeling that every day around her was suddenly my birthday. And, although being able to go only so far with Kelly was tantalizing and frustrating on one hand, such limitation hid the fact that I wouldn't have known what to do with her had I been granted access to her promised land anyway. I simply felt good talking, sharing, and being mesmerized by her warmth and charm.

One afternoon as we sat on The Wall, I summoned up sufficient dopamine-enhanced courage to present her with a poem I wrote, entitled "A Wish." She was careful not to retain full possession of the folded loose-leaf sheet that my heart had penned, and thereby violate her covenant with Resty. But she agreed with my suggestion that just "holding it and reading it to [herself] for a minute" would be okay:

> If I had a wish, it would be Kelly Patino.
>
> If I went with her, I'd take her where she wished to go—anyplace.
>
> I wouldn't just want her lip gloss smeared on my face.
>
> I hope she considers all of the things.
>
> I wish she'd go with me, and see what love brings.

I still recall the dreamy, restrained look in her eyes, as she avoided a direct stare with me for several seconds, looking down at the paper and allowing my affectionate waves to silently wash over her. I knew immediately that, while I might never fully gain access into what was Resty's castle (at least not in the actual world in which we lived), I had already won her heart, where real emotions and fantasies alone were the means of keeping score.

I spent the next week or so distracting myself from my longing for Kelly by entertaining the overplayed, yet nevertheless flattering, affections of Gina DeLucia. Gina was the type of girl who would have Tweeted her thoughts, Instagrammed her food, and chronicled her days via her Snap story if social media had existed then. Gina, after informing me with an adolescent, bossy charm and a kiss on the cheek, that we were now "going out" with each other (a status I happily accepted), she somehow let everyone know we were a pair within just hours after she had decided so.

Gina was the envy of most. She was stunningly attractive and tall, with dark Italian features and long, black hair. She was animated and warm, too, which made her quite the thirteen-year-old catch.

We all knew that her father was one of those old-school Italian types, who didn't believe Gina should spend any time with boys, and he would have surely conveyed his disapproval through whatever means necessary toward any boy who even attempted to round first base and head toward second. This made her even more alluring to me, as her selection of me to be her "boyfriend" meant she felt I was worth her having to tolerate her dad's disapproval. The vowel at the end of my last name did provide a certain ethnically unstated hedge between her father and me. I understood this fact through an unspoken Italian code, even though I had never spoken to him. The closest I even came to meeting Enzo was hearing his immediate and booming disapproval as Gina entered her house one evening six minutes later than she was due. His chastising, broken English lecture began right as she opened the door, as if his angry monologue was somehow wired to the turn of the doorknob.

Gina was nice, and her eight-day attachment gave me an early confidence boost in the Wild West frontier of girls I had just begun to explore. Mostly, though, interacting with Gina served to remind me how my only true interest was in finding a way to be closer to Kelly.

As I made my way to The Wall one Saturday morning to await whatever friends would come around, Kelly strolled down to my pleasant surprise. Normally, she didn't come out so early and would usually be with Resty or her sister.

"Hi." she matter-of-factly greeted me.

"What's up?" I replied, attempting poorly to display my cool mode, puffing clumsily on a Winston Light, yet also conveying a clear curiosity and concern, as I sensed she was troubled.

"Resty and I decided to take a break from each other for now. Not for good! But we seem to just be arguing all the time, so I told him

I wanted a time-out for now."

I felt like I had just been dealt a straight flush in a game of stud that, until four seconds prior, I didn't even know I was playing. I had to be smart, though, as I knew that overplaying my hand might scare her away. My gut feelings also signaled to me that Kelly didn't wander to The Wall that morning or share her woes with me by accident. She wanted me to pick up the pieces of her wounded heart and present a method for reassembly. I mostly listened to her bemoan the frustrations she had continually experienced with Resty in recent weeks. But sensing she had vented most of her mixed feelings and was pretty settled on moving our conversation in a different direction, I decided to raise the stakes.

"Well, I can just see it in your eyes lately that you haven't been as happy as you usually are. I have an idea, which would be really nice for both of us and help keep your mind off of all this stuff," I began, purposefully omitting her now-separated boyfriend's name from my pitch.

"Okay," Kelly replied simply, her pained eyes widening and softening some, as if my words were a soothing and fast-acting tonic to her troubled state.

"Tonight around 8:00, we should leave Jimmy's party and take a walk down through 'Jacob's Ladder' and spend some time at the log."

The log was an optimal spot for sitting side by side and making out, and it was easier and less risky for me to mention the log than the specific reason I thought we should detour there later. I figured Kelly would be more likely to accept my generic and implied terms versus an outright proposition to kiss her just minutes after she disclosed her surprising sabbatical from *You Know Who*.

Twelve seconds or so later, which seemed like an hour and a half to my wishful, yearning, adolescent soul, Kelly exercised her unique position of power over me, a power to affect my emotions like no other event in my life could, in her typically calm and matter-of-fact way, with a simple response.

"OK, as long as I am home by 9:30, and I don't want to tell anyone where we are going." Those poised, potent words of affirmation uttered by Kelly produced the most abundant and intoxicating surge of dopamine my brain had ever experienced and likely ever would. Just like that, Kelly had accepted my bold invitation for some sacred alone time and then added icing on the improbable cake in the form of a request for secrecy of our plans.

"Cool," was all I could muster in response to heaven's manna, awarded to me through Kelly's human form. I imagined she might have expected a more elaborate and enthusiastic response, but I was afraid that if I said anymore, I might have babbled myself into a boyish stupor for hours, thus accentuating the nervous, eager part of me, which was utterly shocked that she was on board. I was also terrified that I would fail miserably at an act, at which, I surmised, Resty must have become expert.

Making a covert escape from our friend Jimmy's gathering was pretty easy because parties at Jimmy's always spilled out into the woods around his family's house. His parents were never home, so our crew often gravitated to what became a sprawling party zone of tapped kegs of beer, classic rock, and girls almost too good to be true. As planned, we ducked out around 8:00 that night, carrying with us our heightened feelings and packs of Winstons. We could hear Led Zeppelin blaring from Jimmy's garage for a good ten minutes as we faded into the woods toward Jacob's Ladder.

The anxiety about whether I was up to the task, never having kissed a girl for longer than two seconds in my life, dissipated quickly, giving way to the warmth and specialness I felt at finally having Kelly to myself in the most intimate of settings. We sat next to each other on the vacant log as if rehearsing a scene in a play that we had acted a dozen times before, she to my right and I closest to the opening to the path, which now served as the only portal between us and other humans. We calmly extinguished our cigarettes, not caring about their effects on our breath, and instinctively turned toward each other.

There was no bumbling of unnecessary words or other nervous tics from either of us. Just bliss. Our heads tilted the right way and I soon realized that playing poker, chess, and understanding baseball were not my only natural talents in life. We remained locked in the most gentle, silky, and tactile merging of lips, mouths, and tongues I could have ever fantasized. I felt like I had just thrown out the first pitch on Opening Day at Yankee Stadium. Right down the middle. No awkward fumbling or accidental bites on this beautiful evening under the darkened canopy of Staten Island stars.

Mr. Sinatra

It Was a Very Good Year

My father bought a brand-new, white Cadillac in 1979, a Sedan DeVille, replacing his 1976 model. This baby was sharp, with a light-blue vinyl top and interior, and shiny, spoked wheels. It even came with a cassette player. Dad's latest Caddie served as the neighborhood envy and perfect escort for family travel in the summer of 1980. My parents took Paul and me (fourteen and twelve) on a few great excursions that season. We drove to Boston to visit our cousins and experienced the clamoring and discordant enthusiasm of Red Sox fans (or the fans of the "pink team from New England," as I prefer to call them). We also went to Lake Bomoseen, Vermont, and stayed at a family friend's lake house.

Paul and I snuck unfiltered Lucky Strikes from my father's numerous packs, pretending to enjoy smoking them while on the lake in a small-engine boat. To our surprise, we were too young to navigate such a boat legally. We learned this fact later that week when we saw a sign at the marina about needing adult accompaniment if under sixteen, which explained why we received our share of astonished looks as we pushed the small, Mercury outboard engine to its hilt on a few occasions, weaving around other boats and creating literal and figurative waves with some of the perennials. What did they expect from New Yorkers anyway?

Among the many new, exciting and enjoyable experiences we shared during our two-week sabbatical from the city was the exposure to a man I never actually met, yet who accompanied us for the entire trip. That summer, as Dad proudly navigated his latest status symbol up and down the New York State Thruway and Massachusetts Turnpike, he introduced Paul and me to Francis Albert Sinatra, or Mr. Sinatra, if you will. In his mid-sixties, he had recently released two amazing album collections, making another of his many epic resurgences over the years. Mr. Sinatra provided the perfect complementary cadence to our happiful journeys. It felt only right that Sinatra's divine crooning, crystal-clear articulation, uncanny and exquisite timing, and indescribable presence should grace the inner confines of our pristine, leather living room on wheels, further enlivening our vacation bliss.

Dad broke in that new cassette player almost exclusively with the melodic perfections of *The Trilogy—Past and Present, Greatest Hits and Greatest Hits Volume II*, and *She Shot Me Down* albums, which collectively provided a delicious cross section of Sinatra at his best. In excitement, Dad would often poke my mom, who sat right next to him in the middle of the front bench seat, pointing out the brilliant vocal nuances that Frank carried out by the dozen to make sure she didn't miss any of them. "You hear that, Maria? How he did that!?" His typical politeness took a backseat to his captivation with Frank as he sometimes poked my mom right out of one of the few naps she took over the last twenty-five years. She would nod in semiconscious agreement, fibbing at times that she actually heard what he pointed out rather than disappoint him or cause him to use the rewind feature—which also delighted him.

While my mom might not have heard every instance of Frank's saintly diction, I certainly did. Sitting in the back right of the car, often with sunglasses on, I could easily hide my enjoyment or even my wakeful status, thus maintaining my feigned disinterest. After all, listening to Sinatra at my age and gender was the equivalent of forfeiting all precious traces of emerging, American masculinity and parental disregard, the value of which necessitated my new infatuation with Frank to remain a secret affair, at least for now.

Throughout my teens, my love and appreciation of the Chairman of the Board grew with me like other adolescent rites of passage, such as telling a girl what I really thought of her—regardless of the outcome. I cared less what people thought of my strong, visceral attachment to a guy who was like an uncle I'd never met but loved and relied on just the same. His songs, which have been referred to as "three-minute movies" because each is a gripping story of its own delivered by the greatest storyteller of our time, became vivid bookmarks of my life, heightened emotional touchstones for all the moments that mattered. Love, triumph, joy, struggle, resilience, injustice, death of the body, or worse, of the soul, were rhythmically personified and poetically framed by Frank's comforting backdrop to my life. My own three-minute movies in life made more sense because of him. I realized then, still a kid, how fortunate I was to follow suit in experiencing the empowering connection that so many had made with this charismatic crooner. I used to be embarrassed, with so many Italian-American men in my family, at how deeply they revered him, affording him the esteemed status ranked beneath their mothers, Jesus, and the Pope—and usually in that order. That was, until I allowed myself to feel the warmth, familiarity, and comfort Ol' Blue Eyes was born to provide.

A few months after my dad passed away in 1988, about eight years after he had baptized me with Francis Albert, the gaudy Cadillac serving as church, my brother Gerard decided that my Confirmation was now in order. He scored tickets to Frank, Liza Minelli, and Sammy Davis Jr., who were performing at the Meadowlands Arena across the bridge in New Jersey. Frank was pushing seventy-three, and my brother decided to seize the moment, and he did so in the way both he and Frank often did things—with style. Gerard, his girlfriend, and I were picked up by a limousine, and we dressed the part: black suits and ties for the guys and a sizzling, black dress on his girlfriend to match. The three of us were completely sober that evening, but we felt higher than I can explain, floating our way over the Goethels Bridge in another sacramental Cadillac. We knew that those tickets bought us lifetime membership into an exclusive club for those privileged enough to see Sinatra live.

The crowd sat more quickly than for a regular performance given by mortals. We knew that missing even a few seconds of Frank would be sinful. I wondered who would sing first or whether they'd begin with a combination. Liza entered with a booming energy and pipes to match. She did her job, raising the already-dizzying excitement and anticipation felt throughout the packed arena. She was amazing in her own right; yet everyone, including Liza, recognized that even the best antipasto was still a prelude to the main dish.

Thirty minutes later, Sammy followed. Still no sign of Frank, to the tortured delight of the entire audience. While we were squirming in our seats with joyful eagerness, waiting a little longer to see Frank meant an extension of the minutes before we would have to part with him, a permeating thought I preemptively registered. I was already sad that it would be over soon and it had hardly even begun. Sammy, who had the widest breadth of talent among the legendary trinity, dazzled us. He bellowed ballads, joked, and smoked up and down the stage, varying tempo and our moods at his will. His slow and somber rendition of "Mr. Bojangles," perhaps his signature song, complete with a chair on stage, which he gracefully danced around, was riveting. Then, as we were finally about see the former Kid from Hoboken, New Jersey, return (now in his twilight), intermission was announced.

Few people left their seats during the break. Those who risked leaving for a refreshment or restroom visit poured back in frantically at the first flickering of the lights, the visible signal that *he* was coming on. Seconds later, as Mr. Sinatra strutted out to a plethora of flashbulbs and a rousing of sentimental applause, the depth of which was uniquely palpable, I understood what his oft-lauded presence was all about. We were mesmerized, like children seeing Santa for the first time. The communication among the three of us was nonverbal, consisting of the most heartfelt, intermittent smiles, the kind you see on the faces of admiring family watching a bridegroom in their ceremony. We didn't dare taint the moment with the inadequacy of spoken language. Frank provided the communication for us. Early into his half-hour of seduction, his seventy-two-year-old voice cracked for a moment, and before the audience could even wince on his behalf, he joked it away without missing a beat or a note. He simply took things down a notch, adjusting his range and our moods accordingly, reminding us that he would do things his way, and our job was just to enjoy being there.

I thought about my dad as I absorbed the sounds, sights, and charismatic buzz of Sinatra. I lamented how, unlike with me and Frank, I never expressed my love and appreciation for my father openly. Nor did my father for me. That's how we were. My sadness was brief, giving way to the emotionally uplifting command Frank was exerting on me and 20,000 others. I felt like Dad was there anyway, somehow, in the gestures, cockiness, and intensity that was Frank. If my dad had been there in the flesh, watching with us, without the need for a cassette player, I would have been the one enthusiastically poking him to take note of Frank's nuanced mastery. *Did you hear that? Did you see how he...?*

Frank helped me grow up, first by bridging the generational rift between me and my parents, then offering lifelong, enchanting instruction in the enormity of love, the crushing depths of heartbreak, and everything in between. He made it easier to laugh daily in heartfelt joy and to feel utmost dignity in the darkest depths of loss. He not only gave me permission to cry at each end of the emotional pendulum, but he made sure I did so through his irresistible incantations.

Thanks for the Memories, Mr. Sinatra.

G

(1957-1989)

My oldest brother Gerard was everyone's favorite. My Aunt Sue often unabashedly proclaimed this to him and the rest of us. My sister, Carmela, was the firstborn, 1956, born eleven months before Gerard. Joseph arrived eighteen months after him and was his closest peer in life. Paul and I followed, comprising an additional set of DiCristo boys a handful of years later. We never objected to Aunt Sue's inequitable position. We understood and agreed with it. It was plainly obvious to all of us, like admitting spaghetti and meatballs was better than lasagna—that's no knock on lasagna, spaghetti is just *better*. Of course, Gerard was Aunt Sue's favorite. He had an indescribable, bright smile, accentuated by a slightly pronounced front tooth, the result of taking a fastball on his upper lip one spring during Little League. What was a mark of character on "G," as he was affectionately called, might've been seen as a blemish on an average guy, like a ding on a '57 Cadillac. And that was only one of a hundred qualities that made G magnetic, the person everyone gravitated to.

G was also restless, easily distracted, and often bored. He didn't like school when growing up. Today, a boy with his temperament would be flagged as having ADHD or some related disorder (which might have helped him, despite contemporary overdiagnosis of childhood behavior). Instead, he was saddled with unaddressed, latent guilt over consistently underachieving in school. He also struggled with intermittent problems with authority and structure.

Nevertheless, his boisterous and tender charisma, enormous and captivating brown eyes, and thick, black hair mesmerized everyone. Relatives, teachers, other kids, and, eventually, a procession of beautiful girls and women became enamored with him. They responded partly to his striking looks—a naturally muscular, balanced physique, and a symmetrical, pleasing face that glimmered like new pennies. Still, his magnetism was more profound than a reflection of his good looks. G made warm connections with others without effort. Nobody had a choice in the matter; once he locked them in a stare and smiled at them, their hearts met. He was genuine and craved deep, personal connections. That's the way it was with G.

I learned a lot from him as I was growing up. Ten years my senior, some of his influence was good. Some was anything but positive. His troubles were apparent to me, even as a young boy. He didn't attend college, and remained in The Hamptons after the summer of '77 ended, when the rest of the family returned to Staten Island. He tended bar, gambled on sports, and went on lockdown with his then-girlfriend through the winter in a summer town. Both of them drank excessively. Part of me feared his volatile lifestyle and what might happen to him, especially since I often heard my parents' late-night lamentations about him being "off track" and "not making anything of himself." This was troubling to my psyche, of course, but my positive connection to him (and I suppose a self-administered dose of denial about his problems) balanced my worries with feelings of connection, empowerment, adventure, and fun.

G was my first mentor on girls. He taught me how to know when they were likely to "fool around," and how exploring these possibilities as soon as possible was more than advisable. He taught me how to gamble on football games, including "taking my bets" weekly, when I was ten—fifty cents a game, plus the five cents "vig" on losses. And he gave me the scoop on the neighborhood, from the kids and their families to the *connected* people who ran the gambling rings and other illicit activities.

Despite the fact that his influence on me accelerated some of my own eventual problems with substance abuse and bouts of problem gambling, we shared a fraternity and coolness that went a long way toward the formation of my positive character and depth. We watched a thousand Yankee games together, and we shared an emotional codependency on the team. Our moods were tied directly to their latest result on the field, as mine still are today.

One of my favorite sacred rituals of ours was making fun of our grossly overweight, repetitious relatives at family gatherings. We'd laugh uncontrollably at how our aunts and uncles seemed like old, morbid Italian statues, frozen, except for the movements they needed to shove vats of food into their gaping mouths as they murmured bastardized Italian expressions from the Old Country, shifting their food from cheek to cheek. He would sometimes make polite small talk with them, cursing them out under his breath for the fun of it (definitely, if they were too absent-minded to hear him). G always cracked me up; I felt especially significant for being the private audience of such secret, hilarious mockery. We timed how many seconds Cousin Vito would take between twirls of spaghetti as he intently ferried pasta from his plate to his mouth. Seven seconds was his average twirl-to-twirl time, which was second only to Uncle Sal's. He came in at just under six seconds, never taking his crooked eye off the plate in fear that it may vanish if he looked away. We postulated that his eye probably went crooked from this repeated action over the years. There was Robin (*Robeen*), who was supposedly engaged to our cousin, "Little" Anita; their engagement was running for seven years when I got the last update in 1984. Robin drank himself into a Rémy Martin stupor every holiday, which G and I concluded was an understandable reaction to the horrific realization that he might eventually wind up marrying Little Anita, who, incidentally, was not little at all and as crazy as a loon. And so it went, from Uncle Frank's cigar-smoking apathy to the dozens of dark moles on Aunt Maria's face. There was a comedic commentary G and I exclusively shared. Only occasionally would we permit others, such as our siblings, to see an excerpt or two from our "show," pointing out some of the more hilarious idiosyncrasies of our buffoonish relatives. But the main acts were off limits to everyone else; they were only for us.

G also had a beautiful capacity for love and empathy toward those in life who were, as he might have said, "a little off from the rest of us." This was a cardinal trait he possessed. Regardless of what personal crisis he may have been suffering, he would often find a way to show love to other human beings. One example I'll always cherish occurred when he walked a few blocks every morning to catch the express bus to Manhattan for work. He was in his early twenties (working at one temporary, unsatisfying job or another). He met a mentally handicapped man named Henry, who lived a few doors down from us with his parents, and, as G naturally did, he sensed Henry could use a friend more than most. Henry also walked to the bus stop to go work at a group home for a few hours a day, and began to wait before leaving until Gerard came by each morning, so he could join his new friend in the walk. The thing about Henry was he walked sluggishly. He shuffled his feet, perhaps due to his cognitive development and years of taking medication, which meant Gerard missed his bus on more than a few occasions. There was no way he would ever have left Henry behind, though. Jobs came and went. Connections like the one G shared with Henry were essential. He would rather arrive late for work.

Once, he invited Henry over to our home, and Ma cooked a great dinner. Everybody received Henry as if he were a visiting feudal prince. The happiful expressions I saw on Henry's face that entire night as we doted on him, his simplest and widest smiles—full of malformed teeth and a shaky jaw—made an everlasting impression on my heart and soul. In response to our hospitality, Henry repeated his name several times after our first introduction with an obvious, beaming pride.

"I'm Hennnryyyyyyyyyy Craaaaaiiig Juuuuunior," he said.

As a young boy, I couldn't help but laugh as he clumsily elongated his name. But I felt the intense gravity of the evening. I recognized the dignity and honor my family offered him over plates of rigatoni (served because my mom suspected spaghetti might be difficult for him to manage). Arranging to give people like Henry a seat at the table was natural for G; it was part of his character.

There were also incidents when G provided the kind of help that only a big brother can offer, like when I got in trouble for gambling through a guy named Dick. Dick (twenty-five) took my bets on his own account through a local bookie. I was only seventeen, but I had lost several hundred dollars in a week, which resulted in a dedicated physical beating from Dick. While I was in the wrong for betting with him in the first place, his handling of the situation was far more egregious, especially by the norms of our subculture. A kid should have been handled differently. Less than one full day after I came home with multiple facial bruises and obvious swelling from the one-sided fight, G and a friend of his paid Dick a visit. They showed up at his workplace in midtown Manhattan as he left for the day. When he entered the revolving door to exit his office building, G and his friend immediately burst in and joined him in the small compartment, stopping the door from making its circle until they were done. Suffice it to say, Dick paid his own debt that afternoon. My big brother had to ice his hand all night after handling that situation on my behalf. Even though Dick lived only two blocks away from us, I never heard from or saw him again.

Unfortunately, throughout my mid-teens, Gerard and I began to parallel each other on our problematic journeys. He descended into full-blown addictions to gambling, cocaine, and vodka. I struggled with my own brief, yet serious, stints of substance abuse and problem gambling. I was able to break free of both by age eighteen, thanks to some timely intervention from my parents, who connected the dots well enough to point me in the right direction of help.

This turning point in my life served as a catalyst for my decision to explore the helping profession as a career in my early twenties. Ironically, I applied some newly learned skills into organizing a family intervention for G. The technique (now a household word and popularized TV series) was new, and it required my best selling skills to convince my parents and siblings to arrange it. It was even harder convincing Gerard, as we took a "tough love" stance in cornering him to get immediate help.

"We have something to discuss," my mother told Gerard, asking him to sit down on the one open spot on the corner of the couch, with the rest of the family sitting, silently around the living room. Staging G's seat to be in the corner of the room farthest from the door, was intentional. It was one of many subtle, key orchestrations I arranged for the intervention.

"Each of us has something to say, and all we ask is that you listen," Ma instructed Gerard, employing an infrequent, somber tone that commanded respectful obedience and conveyed no interest in an immediate rebuttal from her son.

The intervention began with my brother Paul, who, although certainly close with G, was the least emotionally attached, thus a safer choice to break the ice. An individually prepared list was read aloud to G, detailing how his drinking and drug use had specific negative effects on each person present. Care was given by everyone to avoid sounding too harsh in presenting the facts, but we wanted to ensure that the hurt caused by his troubling behavior was not soft-pedaled. At the close of each list, as designed, each family member conveyed a desire in their own way that G would get help for his problems. While he rolled his eyes, grimaced, and squirmed in his seat through six iterations of one truth—that he was falling apart and in desperate need of help, I could see his openness to surrendering his failed attempts to make things right growing by the minute. The final list was read by our mother, who took extra care to underline the fact that while she wasn't angry with G, she was at wit's end and expected him to finally take action to correct his path.

"Here's the deal, G," I interjected before he was about to respond to Ma's closing imploration. "Dr. Frank [our cousin] has arranged a bed at the detox unit in Staten Island Hospital. It's ready now, and we can drive you down there. You don't need to take much with you. Ma already started packing your bag. After detox for a few days, where all you do is nothing except eat and give yourself a few days to relax, there will be another place lined up outside of the city. We're finalizing the details as to where that place will be, but the idea is, you'll get a chance to reset and learn some ways to overcome your shit when you come back, just like I did, without having the temptations of the people, places, and things in the neighborhood."

"What about Linda?" G feebly inquired, referring to his girlfriend, who was not present. He could sense he was "losing this hand."

"All good," I replied, "In fact, she'll be here in a few minutes to drive you to the hospital." My oldest brother, who served as my mentor in manipulation, couldn't help but smile at the irony. How could I, his little brother, have pulled such a "move" on him with this whole intervention thing?

Minutes after our loving ambush, he was off to detox. Days later, he entered a wonderful treatment environment in Upstate New York, which was run by a married couple in their forties out of their farmhouse. Mitch and Mary had overcome their own battles with alcoholism and codependency years earlier in the city, and they had created this homey refuge in the country to dedicate their lives to helping others do the same.

After his time at the farmhouse, G never drank, did drugs, or gambled again. He spent the better part of the next two years gratefully applying what he had learned about living a sober life to helping others do the same. At last, his gregarious nature and uncanny ability to bond with anyone flourished, unhampered by the personal weight of teenage troubles or adult addiction. In this instance, my big brother followed his little brother into a renewed world of positivity and "recovery." It was an unlikely, amazing, and inspirational turn of events, as he seemed to finally gain a sense of stability and purpose, which had always eluded him.

Unfortunately, these welcomed tides of hope were short-lived, and life took an abrupt and dreadful turn for the worse. G still struggled to detach himself from a handful of former associates who spent their lives chasing dollars and excitement in all the wrong ways. Although G remained true to his newfound sobriety, where gambling, drinking, and substance use were concerned, his weakness to the allure of fast money—"making moves," as we often called it—tragically caught up with him. Our mother often said that water seeks its own level. Sadly, it did so in his case.

Nearing twenty-one, I decided to move out of our family home in Staten Island to another town a hundred miles upstate. I planned on continuing college there while working as a substance abuse counselor and figuring out the next steps in life. I felt highly enthusiastic about branching out from my family to chart my own course, but I also felt somewhat saddened at leaving. My father had died less than a year before; he was only fifty-eight. And, although his failing health issues gave us some warning, his death in February of 1988 came much quicker than any of us expected. Naturally, I had mixed feelings about moving away from my grief-stricken mother.

In addition to moving, I had begun to distance myself from G emotionally over the months prior to moving out. I got the sense he was risking his own well-being by living dangerously with characters I saw as rotten apples. I told him I was concerned about him and where he was heading, but, I had to get out of Staten Island for my own personal growth. I knew by his nonverbal, conciliatory response to my admonitions, he understood fully. He wasn't upset with my position. I also knew that, in his mind, he was hoping and rationalizing how he only needed to "make a few more moves," so he could accumulate enough cash to free himself from his current lifestyle and leave Staten Island. The sociopathic leeches that G hung around were a stain of our

Italian-American subculture that we had to deal with, but they were part of our culture both then and now. I doubted whether he would ever truly cut ties, and feared he was more likely heading for an overt, potentially catastrophic relapse in addictive behavior. Concerned as I was for G's well-being, I ultimately knew I could not control his actions. What I didn't know, at least not consciously, was that our distanced and uneasy conversation about his path was the last one we would ever have on Earth.

I moved to Kerhonkson, in New York's Hudson Valley, in mid-January of 1989. Given that my birthday was soon approaching and I was sure to miss my family immediately, I planned to return for a quick, three-day stay beginning Tuesday the twenty-fourth, during which we would celebrate my birthday on Wednesday, the twenty-fifth. After a busy ten days getting settled in my new, one-bedroom apartment and learning some ropes at my new job, I drove to our family's home after my 11p.m. late shift. It was about a two-hour drive, which was fun and relaxing for a night owl like me, especially after eight hours of interaction with addicts in a residential treatment setting. I was feeling accomplished, proud of myself for my recent transition, and I was excited to fill my family in on the details.

As I climbed the outside stairs to our house, I saw that the light was on in G's basement bedroom. He wasn't home, I also noticed when looking in his window. I knew he was on the dating scene at that point and not working standard hours. So I wasn't concerned that he was out at 1 a.m. The next morning, however, as I caught up with Ma over coffee, I learned that no one had heard from him since about eight o'clock the night before, when he had assured my mom that he would be back shortly.

Among all the scenarios that crossed my mind, none was good. While it didn't quite fit in my deepest sense of logic, I imagined that he finally relapsed on cocaine and was strung out in a hotel somewhere, unable to communicate while he finished his bender. I was also sensing something worse, because he knew I was coming home to visit and would have done his best to show up, even if he were actively fighting off demons. As that dreary winter Wednesday dragged on, my mom, sister, and I began to share a growing dread that something bad had happened. My intuition reached for the worst outcomes imaginable among the three of us, probably because I had the most acute understanding of his recently wayward path.

Nevertheless, I hoped, now prayed, he was as high as a kite somewhere and too embarrassed to face us. We made some inquiries with his "friends," poked around the neighborhood some, but as they say, "nobody knew nothin'." As the eerie hours of that Wednesday evening passed, thoughts of my birthday celebration evaporated into a vapid hole of deafening silence and unmentionable dread.

I was scheduled to work that Thursday afternoon, January twenty-sixth, all the way back upstate. Despite G's unknown whereabouts, a part of me still planned to return on time, reasoning there wasn't much more I could do at that point. The police had been informed, and we could only hope and wait. It was probably more of a subconscious force tugging at me to leave, as if my leaving might help this increasingly awful dread vanish. A couple hours before I was set to begin my drive back, I was struck by a gut feeling that necessitated action. I sought out a couple of guys he knew, hoping to investigate whether they knew anything about his whereabouts on Tuesday evening, the last time my family saw him. I drove to a local bar before noon and asked Fat Jim and Joey Blue, two wannabe "wiseguys" who were already drinking, what they knew. Jim said he thought G was heading to South Beach Tuesday night, a nearby neighborhood. I stared into Jim's and Blue's eyes to ascertain whether they knew more than they were leading on, and was satisfied that they did not. I did read in their body language, though, that they had arrived at the same calculation I was now quickly reaching. None of us needed to say it aloud.

South Beach isn't a large area, but it's more than a few blocks. Ironically, as I drove down the first random street in the vicinity, perhaps now guided by a divine compass, I immediately spotted G's parked car. It was a new, candy-apple-red El Dorado with a white-leather interior, which he had recently bought through a "friend" who helped him get a loan. The car was parked on the right side of the street along a wire fence in front of a vacant lot. Across the street was a row of modest and typical South Beach houses. Fittingly, it was beginning to rain lightly, which made the January air feel even colder. I knocked on a door and asked to use the phone to call my sister, Carmela, who was home with our distraught, hopeful mother. She left to meet me after calling the police to meet us at the scene. The guy who let me use the phone mentioned that he first saw the car there Tuesday evening, and that he didn't think it had been moved since, which was now about forty hours ago.

Carmela arrived quickly and we awaited the cops. The January, New York rain, cold and biting just moments ago, no longer felt like anything. I was suddenly impervious to all sensations other than a pulsating heart infused with bolts of adrenaline. As we awaited the police, sharing a silent, desperately fading hope that horror was not upon us, my subconscious conclusions began to break through my awareness like bulls at a rodeo. I circled the area and talked silently to myself in a surreal attempt to prepare for what cannot be prepared for, straying a few feet away from Carmela, who stood in dreadful worry by the car, perhaps beginning to sense the fate she was instinctively standing guard over. I didn't know that Carmela had an extra key for the El Dorado with her; I figured the cops would open the car when they arrived. Thank God, I didn't know she had that key, because the traumatic and sickening event would have been even more obscene if we discovered it alone.

The cops arrived and asked us if we had already opened the trunk. Carmela said no and handed them the key. In a defensive move, driven by abject fear and an instinctual grasp at psychological survival, I quickly stepped back from the trunk to the front of the car so I could not see inside the trunk as it was opened. One officer opened it and then closed it in a nearly solitary motion. Both cops then glanced at each of us, now standing like rooks on a chess board at the front ends of the car. No words were necessary.

I looked upward and silently consulted with God. *It's one thing for Dad to go, but now this? I can't let this take me down. I've faced enough challenges and loss in life,* I thought. I was determined in my core to remain strong. After those five seconds or so of my heavenward focus, where time briefly stopped and sound was inaudible, a hellish explosion of grotesque noises shrieked me back into full awareness. Carmela was screaming in inarticulate and inconsolable disbelief. The cops began putting yellow tape around the perimeter of the car. In a flash, a local newspaper reporter was on the scene and taking pictures. Cops were asking us questions. Neighbors were now gathering in morbid curiosity, and the beginning of the end of Gerard DiCristo had happened.

Carmela violently yanked a large camera away from a newsman and barked obscenities at him, his publication, and the world, refusing to give it back. I had a passing thought of how I wished I could have done something to help her. But I knew that the best I could do was keep my cool and prevent any further destruction of whatever psychological fragments were still shielding my heart. An ambulance arrived, and the medics convinced Carmela to sit down inside of the back of it and talk with them. From twenty feet away, I could see the fear in their eyes that they might be unable to stabilize her.

She complied, though, with the "piece-of-shit-bastard" reporter's camera still in her hand, and I was relieved that she at least had someone attending to her. One of the cops came over to me in the crowd now standing about fifty feet from the car across the street. He asked if I would be willing to go over and make a positive identification, since no one had done so. He was tactful and reminded me I wasn't required to view the inside of the trunk at that moment, but he was still pressing, like cops do, to produce as many facts as quickly as he could. I don't know how my brain functioned so sharply at that moment from within my utterly traumatic haze, but it thankfully did.

"What is he wearing?" I replied calmly.

"A Celtics jacket," the cop said. Gerard's and my favorite basketball team.

"It's him. Someone else can verify that at another time." I answered matter-of-factly.

Thankfully, an inner compass of sanity didn't allow me to consider that it could be someone else lying shot dead in that trunk. Whatever infinitesimal chance of that being true, I knew the traumatic effects of having to look in his trunk myself would have been irreparable, not worth the one-in-a-billion odds. I was good with numbers, and I knew it was my brother.

After the scene stabilized some, Carmela willingly handing over the camera, and I discussing some practical matters with the cops, I knew we had to go home and break the news to my mom. I'll never forget how I managed to drive my car, with Carmela in the passenger seat, the mile or so home, both of us still in a complete mind-and-body-numbing state of shock. When I stopped at a red light, it all felt surreal, so traumatic that I couldn't help but contemplate the scene for a moment, as if it were happening to two other people. I then refocused my mind and began rehearsing how we would shortly enter our home together and share the grisly burden of telling our mom. But when we parked in front of our house and exited the car, I couldn't do it. I stopped walking at the three lower stairs, which preceded another set of stairs outside the house.

"You gotta tell her," I said to Carmela, as I feebly attempted to stabilize my fractured nerves by sitting on the ground.

I then heard two utterances I'll never forget. As she entered the front door, Carmela, in a steady tone, attempting to provide whatever layer of psychological cushion possible, told my mother:

"Gerard is with Daddy now."

A few seconds later, during which Carmela must have elaborated, I heard a wincingly loud moan from somewhere inside my mom's shattering body, the likes of which I never heard before, not even in movies. The second grenade had exploded in our home in less than a year, and this blast had more power, more shrapnel, than my father's premature death.

One week after finding him, the funeral was complete, and the burial was carried out next to my father's headstone, which Gerard had helped design. As Gerard was lowered next to it, we saw my father's engraving for the first time—it felt pathetic, morbidly ironic. The initial, ineffective attempts to console one another made the misty, cold, soul-dampening rain compound the funeral's gloom.

I packed the last few miscellaneous items into my car, which I had left behind a month earlier when I left my home. It was time to resume what I had begun a few weeks earlier, to find my own way, to make my mark. This journey upstate would be different, however, as would every journey in my life to come. After navigating the early loss of my father, the second of two principal male influences in my life, my thirty-one-year-old big brother, G, was also gone.

Murdered. Snuffed out. Vaporized.

Two Dollars Per Smile

A Joy Doubled

It is a beautiful November morning as I drive out of the small town of Amherst, Massachusetts, toward Boston to fly back home to Newport Beach after a Thanksgiving visit with my daughter. The brisk, New England air had chilled my rental SUV overnight, making the first few miles quite sobering, especially since whenever it's cold, I always remove my black leather jacket before taking the wheel. I guess I'm a little OCD like that; having too many layers on bothers me.

I always feel sad when I depart from visiting one of my daughters, knowing that our geography makes spending time together less frequent than I would wish for. No satellite radio yet or fumbling for my organic walnut halves or perfectly farmed organic apples from my black Tumi attaché case on the seat to my right. Just a few, rare moments of rumbling reflection under the glistening cloudless sky. The solitude of the moment prompts my ruminations to deepen. I feel a bit heavy thinking about my daughter's well-being: whether I am doing enough to help her navigate her twenty-five-year-old, frenetic life, or if I am perhaps already meddling more than I should. Anxiety wins a few moments of my heart as I mentally stray, considering turbulence at work, future aspirations, the most recent Match.com hopeful, my other daughter's state of being, and where I should eat dinner after I land in Orange County, California. I debate the merits of finding a cup of coffee before hitting the freeway, weighing the fact that my caffeine level is uncomfortably low against having to make a restroom stop along the way.

"First-world problems," I joke aloud to myself, recalling the dozen times my daughter and I recited that anchoring mantra over the last four days, discussing a myriad of topics from the innocuous and pervasive phenomenon of white, male privilege to how it really must suck for the unfortunate kids from Massachusetts to grow up as Red Sox fans without ever getting proper Yankees exposure.

My mood now leveling back in the familiar direction of feeling pretty grateful about mostly everything in life and with the inside of the Hyundai Santa Fe warming comfortably, I spot a Dunkin' Donuts on my left, so I decide to commit to coffee. After weaving through the roped lines, which remind me of going through security at Logan

Airport, I emerge at the left side of the counter just as a headset-wearing, uniformed employee arrives on the other side.

"Good morning, sir! What can I get for you today?" a smiling woman of twenty-something inquires gleefully.

"Hi, good morning! Small coffee with cream please," I reply with enthusiasm, wanting to mirror her cheer in appreciation.

"Will that complete your order for today?"

"Yes, thank you."

"That will be one-seventy-five please."

I always carry an old-school wad of cash, arranged with all the heads lined in the same direction and the smaller bills on the outside, progressing in value within the stack. I flip past a few singles and hand her a two-dollar bill.

"Wow! That's a two-dollar bill. Cool!" the gregarious counter-woman exclaims, smiling at me as if to confirm my realization that I had just parted with something spectacular.

"I know it is. That's why I gave it to you," I reply, returning a smile and feeling glad that she was so tickled over something so simple. I had come to learn that most people didn't realize that this curious denomination of Americana, first issued for the Bicentennial in 1976, was still readily available at most banks and could simply be ordered if they happened to be out. Her reaction is especially exuberant and infectious this morning, though, and completes my positive mood swing.

"Hey, Linda, this guy just gave us a two-dollar bill," she shouts toward the back of the kitchen at her coworker. As she continues to beam gratefully in my direction, now engaging a drive-through customer via her head-set, I feel compelled to augment her happifulness. I reach back into my front left pocket and take out my pile of green, thumbing quickly to the twos that remain and drop two of them on the counter. Not wanting to disturb her communication with her customer, I simply gesture my head toward her and then toward the back at her colleague, signaling my intention for each of them to have one bill. No further words are exchanged. We share a mutual, sacred glow toward each other instead. I turn and leave the store, feeling the cool air on my face. It really is a beautiful morning.

The Jews

Pangs of Ignorance

On occasion, my boyhood Saturday walking adventures around Fortieth Street would involve an encounter with "The Jews." That's how we, "The Italians," myopically referred to the community of Hasidic Jews who lived in the Boro Park section of Brooklyn. As a young boy, I didn't realize how much prejudice existed between us, or even what the word prejudice meant. But having grown up rarely hearing the word "Jew" unmodified by an attached pejorative, I sensed that the Hasidic families in our neighborhood certainly weren't on the approved list of neighbors.

They, of course, weren't the only ethnic group we stood at odds with.

"The spics," my family would say, (Puerto-Ricans and all other brown people whose actual country of origin didn't even warrant the effort to distinguish, let alone name) "are not to be trusted and are likely to rob you. That's just how they are."

"The blacks," ("niggers" was not a generally acceptable term, yet was warranted when "they" did something overtly wrong) "are a whole different group *altogether.*"

Common descriptions of black kids in our Italian family posse, ones we would offer while seeing ourselves as polite in the process, would routinely include qualifiers, such as "He picks things up in school pretty well for a black kid," or "She's not as loud as you would think she would be"—benevolent "compliments" offered toward those who we understood to be "less than," even though we didn't view their statuses on the lower rungs of humanity as being their fault.

"The Irish," (the only other kind of acceptable white people we felt needed identification) "are OK, provided they aren't too drunk."

And the Asians...

"Well, there's no need to even mention them."

In fact, I can't recall ever speaking with a "chink." The Jews, though, maintained the position of being the catch-all group most easily despised and sanctioned for ongoing overt acrimony.

The vitriol that my family routinely dispensed at the Jews went far beyond bad language and unstated disgust on one ugly occasion. When I was six, my brother Joseph, then fifteen, summoned me to the window of his bedroom to witness an advanced display of his Jew hatred. He had carefully fashioned a metal paper clip into a sharp, pointed mini-spear of sorts, bending open one end of the sharp clip to expose its serrated and potentially dangerous edge, and sliding a rubber band inside the remaining coiled portion of the clip, thereby creating a makeshift slingshot, which could propel the weaponized clip by pulling back and then releasing the band. I thought he was merely "playing around" with me when he first displayed this homemade weapon. He wasn't, though.

Joseph pointed it out the back window, two backyards down, where a handful of Jewish kids were playing, and took a shot. The kids scattered instantly, taking cover on their own property or running inside their home.

My mind still denied the growing possibility of what had occurred. That is, until the doorbell rang a few minutes later. My mother, who had been in the kitchen, oblivious to Joseph's terroristic doings twenty feet from her, descended the long stairway to the ground floor, and greeted a Jewish woman. Joseph and I crept down a few steps to look on, and I'll never forget what I witnessed.

The mother, hysterical and tearfully enraged, had her son in tow. She pulled him by the hand and turned him around toward my mom in order to show her the metal clip still half-lodged behind his knee, blood drips visible down his leg.

My mom was shocked and struggled to say anything through her mortified posture of shame and horror at her son's deviant, harmful behavior. The two mothers exchanged communication through mostly gestures, a kind of surreal, unspoken body language, which my six-year-old mind translated as an apology from my mother, with an implied promise to address Joseph in some way over this, and an approval by the injured boy's mother of my mom's remorse and professed intentions. Despite her own tensions around dealing with the Jews, my mother disciplined Joseph, I imagined, and I suspected that my father was summoned to add some moral authority and a leather belt. But the issue was never discussed among our family, so whatever my parents' course of action was, addressing the abuse of the boy still didn't earn the dignity of a public address, not even at our dinner table.

I also found their uniform garb of black suits and hats for men, curls and beanies for the boys, and drab dresses and funny hair (wigs) by the women uncomfortable and strange. My childish understanding was left to its limited devices, unaltered by any positive information to the contrary from the adults in my life. Hence, I felt particularly uneasy around this subset of neighbors, as if always poised to have an argument with any Jew I saw. Thankfully, one incident, in particular, added a different perspective to my still highly impressionable psyche.

During one of my Saturday walks to Tony's Candy Store around the block, which involved walking by a row of Jewish houses, a Hasidic man quickly scaled the steps of his home as I walked by. He asked me for some assistance—to come inside and shut off an air blower because neither he nor his family members could touch it. I understood why. It was the Sabbath, as observed in Jewish orthodoxy from sundown Friday to sundown Saturday. During this time, Jews are forbidden to operate any modern machinery or electronics. On the rare occasion when a family may have forgotten to shut off an air conditioner or other gadget the night before, a non-Jew like me would be summoned to assist. Even at age six, I could sense through his demeanor his ambivalent tension in asking me to help.

I also observed the notably curious body language of his children, who stood cautiously, several feet behind him, in awe—and perhaps even afraid—that he was talking to me. Two young girls, maybe ages three or four, stared at me. And a boy, around my age, stood in a protective posture in front of them, making clear eye contact with me, demonstrating his version of a cultural warrior pose—which I keenly understood as I met his stare with an "Italian" glare of my own. An interruptive yet short-lived train of thought arose—rooted in a pang of youthful and tender conscience—that I should engage my three fellow youngsters, reaching through the invisible, undeniably real gate separating us. It vanished, however, amid the pressing dealings between their father and me.

Weighing the angles as best I could—sensing their sincere need for help without my feeling threatened—I accepted his request to intervene and proceeded to follow him into their home. He led me back, as his children followed like goslings behind us, to a floor-mounted air conditioning unit in the bedroom he shared with his wife. He pointed out which switch I should turn, and I did, thus freeing them of an icy bedroom without having to compromise their morals. I imagine he did pay a fee in personal pride, though, having to enlist my help and allowing me to enter a room in which a stranger surely had no business.

I never looked at our Hasidic neighbors quite the same way again. That truthful seed planted by my own firsthand experience with a Jewish family would eventually grow into a wonderful and profound intuition, despite the harsh and poisonous soils in which it first took root. While I knew the city block we shared was a "one way," I started to appreciate how the best roads in life were two way.

Just Jean

Reclaiming My Soul

I was starting to find my way through the morass of dating "gonk" (my daughters coined that word as children, as only little kids can, a kind of catch-all word to include anything difficult, confusing, or frustrating) and I was beginning to stabilize financially. It was the spring of 2012, and I had known Jean for some time via business dealings years prior, and we had always gotten along well. In that capacity, we had only met a few times, which was the extent of our connection.

A true Northern California spirit, Jean was the definition of mellow. She had an evident calmness in her soul that was soothing and inviting to anyone in her vicinity. People near Jean felt accepted, cared for, and unjudged. Having lived through some seriously edgy times in her teens, she welcomed the sense of peace she effortlessly exuded. Her temperament was especially welcomed (in light of my recent personal struggles) when we were reacquainted at a spring business convention. She was also happy to see a familiar face, having gone through her own recent marital separation.

Among her magnetic qualities, perhaps the most striking, was how her iconic beauty assumed a back seat to her genuineness, warm spirit, and staunch loyalty. She was old-school and full of sexy edge, almost steely in demeanor at first. If you treated her with respect, as I did, you would quickly be rewarded with a true friend who "had your back," as she might say. So it didn't take more than a few minutes of afternoon catch-up, facilitated by a few vodkas, for us to begin to mutually acknowledge the visceral connection and potential oasis we sensed in each other. I was bolder than usual—playing with her hair and caring nothing about the reaction of our mutual friend, who had shared a drink with us, or about her potential rejection of my flirtatious advances. I liked everything about her, and the timing couldn't have been better. Her 5-foot, 11-inch, 110-pound frame, dressed in the most sexually casual garb of loose jeans and an unassuming top, complemented her intensely mesmerizing blue-green eyes. Her holistic appeal was multiplied by her unpretentiousness. She was simply lovable.

A few months later, Jean moved nearby in Orange County to start a new personal, professional chapter in her life. We became pals initially and lovers soon after—a process that enveloped my body and soul like no experience I ever had. I loved her in no time, in all the ways I had not been fully aware of prior. I was spiritually, emotionally, and physically drawn to her, and felt like home in her presence. I had heard about how simply watching TV with someone—if it's right—could feel intoxicating and satisfying. Well, it was true. *Shark Tank* and *Wicked Tuna* were never so entertaining until Jean. Truthfully, I would have watched static on the screen to be connected with Jean—my newfound Sherpa on what I anticipated would be my overdue trek through Heaven on Earth.

When she was busy one evening, I had a free night and went to see a movie alone, something I enjoy doing from time to time. I saw a French film, *Rust and Bone*, with subtitles. In hindsight, I think the potency of the message was likely even stronger without having the familiarity of my native language to dull the bigger meaning. A young woman, who was finding her way in life, worked a second job as a dancer in a seedy bar. When a man treated her badly one night, another guy stepped in to defend her. They befriended each other in the midst of their chaotic lives. A time later, the woman suffered a terrible accident and lost both of her legs above the knees. For a brief time in the film, I didn't know what his reaction would be. Before seeing how he was undeterred by her handicap, I found myself taking a bit of a morbid, yet ultimately wonderful, mental excursion. I imagined what would happen if Jean had suddenly lost her legs in an accident.

A stirring in my soul occurred, an unmitigated love that I had never felt before. I was flooded with thoughts about the practical matters of such a scenario and how I could address them, such as Jean's current apartment being on the third floor, and how we would have to get her one on the first floor. She could still work as she currently did, because she was in online marketing and worked from home. As I saw him carry her on the screen, before she eventually got prosthetics and learned to walk, I thought that I might have to work out a bit more often to carry my beauty's lanky frame without her worrying about it being difficult.

With tears streaming down my face as I sat solo in the theater, I blissfully realized that, in all those flurries of thought around such an event, I had not once considered whether or not I would leave Jean throughout our imagined crisis. I didn't even think about how my life would be affected. I only considered how I could make things as manageable as possible for her and us. I understood in that moment—beautifully, simply, wonderfully, and joyously—that I loved Jean more than I had ever loved a woman, person, or anything other than my daughters. My soul knew I needed to be with her, and any logic or balanced reasoning in this realm was superfluous.

Jean and I proceeded to simultaneously grow intensely closer and ever more apart over the next year or so. In spirit, we seemed to be what is often referred to as soulmates. We found humor in people's oddities and life's ironies. We both yearned for, and sometimes realized, the simple pleasures in life—she making "potatoes" (as she called a delicious omelet) for me on Sunday mornings, my showing up almost nightly with food and spirits. We would drive along the Coast Highway, share a great meal and a buzz afterward. We understood each other, as we were both on the far end of the quirky scale, and together we deeply felt our experiences of going to hell in life and making a U-turn more than once each. These commonalities ran deep and constituted the strong fiber that weaved our bond.

Sadly though, while we were each finding our way in life in ultimately positive ways, some of our deeper routes were heading in different polar directions. Jean suffered some medical issues and had found comfort in daily pot use—too much comfort for me. She also found solace in being a homebody and resisted regular outings. I empathized with this, especially in light of some of the mental strife that life had thrown at her over the years. But I also needed to connect with the world and find ongoing salvation by engaging with it, rather than retreating. Even these important differences would have been relatively minimal to me in their own rights because I had such a deep love for *my Jean*, which she used to adorably appreciate me calling her. I truly felt OK with having some pretty significant blends of oil and water in our recipe. But something deeper and irreconcilable caused me to walk away.

Jean used to joke about how I needed someone who would do

all that "nicey-nice stuff" for me, someone sweeter and more emotionally attentive than the edges in her personality would allow. At times, her urgings were merely playful and perhaps more inquisitive in nature—trial balloons to see if I actually agreed with the premise—to which I consistently and assertively smirked away any idea that Jean couldn't give me what I needed at the core. I secretly maintained that, while there was some truth in her warnings, I was happy enough at the time. I presumed she would soften in this way and become more affectionate, initiating, and warm. I knew parts of her heart beat to these rhythms, and I figured it was only a matter of time until the rest of her heart ultimately played the whole tune. I was wrong.

As I continued to grow in my ability to truly embrace life with a joyful, grateful, and vulnerable heart, she cooled further. Sadly, she was close to bankrupt emotionally, and her fear of risking an investment brought out the worst in her. The more often and deeply I expressed my need for emotional connection, the further she withdrew, even bristling at times. I'm a bit of a savior at heart, and I don't wish to fully extinguish that streak; however, I had also come to revere and love myself and my heart too wonderfully to continue stepping on this emotional rake in the illogical and futile hope that it might not strike me.

At 3:00 a.m. on a Sunday, after awakening in a dreadful, now unmistakable familiar state of anxiety, I left her bed and my love. Ambling down her apartment steps in a pre-dawn, emotional stupor almost too surreal for description, I knew I had initiated what would be a prolonged and intense phantom pain of my own in cutting myself off from my Jean. But I needed to seek a more compatible partner—one who loved me as I did Jean, or even half as much. Someone who could and would love me back in my own love languages, even in a few of my idiosyncratic dialects.

"To SIL - M.V.P."

Baseball Bliss

It was the summer of 1977. I was nine. My family had recently moved that April to Staten Island from Brooklyn. It wasn't far in miles, hardly across the Verrazano Bridge on the island side. But it marked what I would eventually come to understand as the beginning of the end of my childhood. Those early years were far from ideal. But they did provide a deep sense of familial closeness and unity, facilitated by our geographic proximity to the "old neighborhood." Our move resulted in some anxiety-filled months finishing up fourth grade in a public school for the first time—as opposed to the familiar, structured rules of Catholic school. Because there were no openings in St. Sylvester's, our first summer on Staten Island could not come too soon.

After spending a good part of the summer in eastern Long Island, as we were typically lucky enough to do annually, we had August left to spend in Staten Island before school resumed. Little did I know, I was about to have one of the greatest days of my life.

My parents enrolled my brother Paul and me (just eleven and nine) in a week-long daytime baseball camp. I had recently been "baptized" a year or so earlier into our strong and well-established lineage of diehard Yankee fans, prior to the start of the 1976 season. That season marked the Yankees' first playoff appearance since 1964, so the process of dyeing a big part of my heart and soul an indelible navy blue coincided with the emergence of one of baseball's greatest dynasties to date. Although the Yanks were demolished by the Big Red Machine (the Cincinnati Reds) four games to none in the World Series (thus inflicting one of the deepest wounds on my now-pinstriped psyche) the resurgence of the Yanks was grand and glorious enough to dwarf that pain. It gleefully propelled my instant, growing love for baseball.

At camp that summer, I felt comfortable and excited. I soaked up all of the instruction, mastered the art of holding my back foot in front of first base while making a target for infielders to throw to. I was delighted to learn the nuance and quick thinking necessary to playing first base, the position once graced by Lou Gehrig himself. As an infielder's throw made its way to first, I would either make a "stretch" to receive it safely and as quickly as possible, or leave the bag in case of an errant throw, preventing further advance from the runner. I loved needing to be quick-minded and relying on my baseball instincts, because doing so played into my mathematically gifted mind. For me, camp was an entire week of sacred time.

I wasn't a great hitter, and was slightly smaller than average for my age. I held my own "at the stick," though, and shined brightly on the field, thriving on my rapid development into a heady and fearless player.

While I excelled and relished every moment of playing ball that week, I knew I wasn't as exceptional a player as a few of the kids were. It's funny how, as children, it's easier to perform a simple and honest self-assessment. I guess we are still free of the strong sense of *must's* and *should's* we pick up as we age. I felt OK being a notch above average. I was a solid, sharp player, and like the great DiMaggio, I played stoically, with a deep sense of reverence for the game—a code of honor that required muted emotions on the field and a Catholic-school approach to mastering the game's dogma and liturgy.

Each afternoon at camp, we came in and cooled down in the air-conditioned confines of the clubhouse. We'd watch a thirty-minute film on a World Series while our parents made their way to pick us up. During this time, the best four players of the day were recognized, and each had his name dropped in a hat for a special drawing. The daily winner received a gift and was dubbed Most Valuable Player of the camp that day. Earlier in the week, the Cardinals were in town playing the Mets, so they visited the camp and put on some hitting and fielding displays. They also signed a handful of team baseballs. These became the MVPs' daily prizes.

The fourth day I was there and the next to last day of the camp, I had the kind of day any kid who has ever swung a bat dreams about. As I already knew, I was not on the top rung of talented kids, but this day I was flawless. I made some exceptional diving stops, an unassisted double-play, and I even channeled my inner Reggie Jackson, knocking liners like a Yankee. Even at nine, I knew with every cell of my baseball body and soul that I was unstoppable that day. And my keen, youthful instincts told me I might never have a day like this again. I bathed in the sacredness of every catch, every shuffle of my feet, every effortless, successful swing. I wasn't surprised one bit when my name was announced as one of the four best players of the day during our cooldown.

As a math whiz—numbers being another aspect of baseball that appealed to me—I remained fully aware that, despite my outstanding performance, I still faced three-to-one odds against winning the ultimate prize, the signed baseball. Honestly, I didn't even like the Cardinals. After all, they weren't from New York, and they didn't wear pinstripes. That was that. But it didn't matter. I wanted to win the ball more than anything I could ever remember in the 3,000 days of my existence. And then I won.

"Did they call my name?" I asked one of the boys next to me. I was stunned.

Propelled by boyish joy and exhilaration that even Kevin Costner would be hard-pressed to capture in the movies, I scampered up to the coach, who had drawn my name from the hat. Even the tears of the most-talented boy—his name was entered a few times that week but fell short on the drawing—didn't dim the inferno that was burning in my baseball heart. I paused for a few seconds, recognizing that he was an exceptional player. I considered, in one sense, how his not earning a ball was unfair. I even thought about giving him mine, but that lasted only a few milliseconds. It was an instinctual reflex, a product of my moral upbringing, one I was predisposed to believe was the right one. *I deserve that ball,* I thought. *I need that ball.* I quickly rejected the idea that I should be generous in my moment of glory.

The ball still sits on my bookcase, next to a few copies of Victor Frankl's *Man's Search for Meaning* and my box set of the complete *Little House on the Prairie* series. The signatures are still as crisp as the day they were penned. An inscription in my father's handwriting added the day after, reads: "To SIL – M.V.P." Recounting the smile on his face when he inscribed the ball brings joyful tears to my eyes every time.

Going to Aunt Sue's

A Treat All on its Own

"I need fifty more pignoli in these meatballs before I can bake them for dinner at six," she announced with contagious enthusiasm. It was usually around 2:00 p.m. when she would start her frenetic, daily cooking drills.

"Carrie and John are coming for lunch on Tuesday at 12:30, so I have to defrost some veal cutlets I bought last Thursday from Pete's. Uncle Mickey will pick up some fresh bread on his walk Tuesday morning around 11:00. Right, Mickey?" she asked.

"Yes, Sue!" Uncle Mickey reflexively verified her question from his lounge chair, a habit. It was as instinctual as uttering "and also with you" to the priest at Sunday Mass. He took care to color his reply with a tone of buoyant reassurance, so he wouldn't sound as if he was placating his industrious wife—even though he had probably been asked the same question six times since the night before, when Aunt Sue began her week's advanced planning.

"Paul, Silvio!" Aunt Sue called out to us, forgetting for a moment that we were sitting silently three feet behind her, transfixed by what could have been the female version of *The Galloping Gourmet*.

"As soon as I put the meatballs in the oven at 350 degrees, in about twenty minutes (as if Paul and I needed to know the precise cooking temperature), Uncle Mickey will make some ice cream."

These were the magic words. At the promise of ice cream, Aunt Sue ensured another twenty minutes of cooking time without Paul and me getting too restless. And, in the fashion of a good Italian wife, she had also instructed Uncle Mickey of his next task for that day, providing him ample warning and never asking—simply informing everyone in the non-bossy, matter-of-fact third person.

Looking around the kitchen, something I often found myself doing when taking a break from Aunt Sue's cooking show, I always felt a sense of eeriness. Other than the streaking comet of Aunt Sue's grey-haired vivacity, the kitchen was drab. It was stale, lifeless. The floor was a tired, brown-and-white linoleum, which had long since lost its finish.

The dirt between the seams had turned the white caulk black after accommodating years of Aunt Sue's two-stepping across the floor. There were also several odd-looking items on the shelves above the table, like an oversized pair of retired ceramic salt and pepper shakers, two Franciscans. Their rosy-cheeked smiles and big, round bellies overlooked the kitchen like secret guards. I guess they were grandfathered into protecting the kitchen shelf, even though they no longer seasoned our meals. Aunt Sue kept rubber placemats on the table to "keep rings and stains off the wood," but no one could see much wood through the clutter of recipe books and Aunt Sue's well-worn, personal telephone book. It must have predated the Victrola. There were cut-out grocery coupons strewn about and a pair of scissors for clipping upcoming circulars—her daily ritual. Sitting in Aunt Sue's kitchen always felt like watching an old black-and-white movie, but I was always eager to watch her Oscar-worthy performances.

It was a tight space in Aunt Sue's kitchen, with a small, wooden table pushed against the wall opposite the stove and sink. There were usually only two chairs out, one at each end, where Aunt Sue and Uncle Mickey normally ate. Aunt Sue often seemed like a human magnet, pressed right up to the sink or stove busily preparing a variety of food items, with her back to Paul and me when we sat at the table. She would narrate what she was working on, the back of her red house dress and white apron tie blurring left and right as our eyes followed her like we were watching a tennis volley.

"We're going to Aunt Sue's," Paul and I would say prior to our visits. Deleting Uncle Mickey from the reference was partly instinctual and partly because Aunt Sue was more fun. Growing up in Brooklyn, my brother Paul and I often spent the whole of Saturday at Aunt Sue's and Uncle Mickey's. Aunt Sue was my mother's older sister, who, unable to have her own children, especially enjoyed entertaining us (and my older siblings before us). Since they lived only down the block, as all our relatives did back then, visiting was convenient.

Trips usually consisted of watching their new, 1975 Magnavox television. It was big, bigger than our TV at home, and Uncle Mickey had a "magical clicker." I remember being fully captivated by the hand-sized, black rectangle; its six mystical buttons allowed us to turn the television on or off, increase or decrease the volume, and change any of the seven available channels up or down, one at a time. It could even mute the sound with one push. We liked to press this button while Uncle Mickey slept, listening to the voices on screen cut in and out.

Of course, Uncle Mickey maintained exclusive domain over *The Jetsons* gadget, in fear that we might break it. But when he dozed off, Paul and I "needed to use it," since he was asleep and there was no one to swap the channels between *Bonanza* and *Lost in Space*. Nevertheless, when he was awake, we were sufficiently fascinated to observe him influence the television from his recliner—another prized agent of comfort for Uncle Mickey.

Twenty minutes were up. Aunt Sue's kitchen timer went off, and in went the meatballs. With the closing of the oven door, Uncle Mickey ejected from his lounger and took center stage from Aunt Sue. It was Breyers ice cream time—the Neapolitan kind, stuffed, yet never overstuffed, into a wafer cone. Uncle Mickey walked into the kitchen diligently, with measured steps, the same methodical way he went about everything, and began to clear his spot on the counter. His routine manner was also reflected in his balding grey hair—a uniform, straight-back comb-over. He sported a simple, white tank top (or long-sleeved, collared button down when colder) most days. It was always belted under loose-fitting trousers. Two pairs of black or brown loafers he wore alternatingly. As far as we knew, they were the only shoes he owned.

"Just one cone each," Uncle Mickey announced, as he did every time he prepped for the sweet, methodical ritual, the reward for our non-nagging patience. First, he reached up into the closet and pulled down a long, rectangular box. He carefully opened one of its narrow ends with the steadiness of a brain surgeon. Slowly, and with mesmerizing diligence, he slid out four wafer cones, one at a time, placing each on the counter, far enough from the edge to avoid knocking them on the floor by accident. The box was then carefully returned to its home in the closet. The idea that Uncle Mickey might leave the box of cones out while preparing the ice cream was unimaginable. First things first. So too was the notion of taking the icy box of triple-flavored joy from the freezer before the exact moment it was ready to be opened. The process was scientific. Melting the ice cream was sacrilege.

The scooper was kept in the silverware drawer adjacent to the cutlery, where I suppose it resided for the last quarter-century. Metallic, except for the lime-green handle, it functioned as efficiently as a German automobile, but it was much more important than a Volkswagen to Paul and me. Like well-behaved puppies, we were reminded by "Unc" to give him "room to do [his] work."

"Stay at the table until it's ready," he instructed, placing the rectangular box of Breyers on the counter next to the unfilled cones. Each one was filled with the steadfast precision of a veteran bomb-squad specialist—precisely equal parts vanilla, chocolate, and strawberry. I don't think I ever saw Unc break a cone. Some sculpting followed to all but eliminate the possibility of a spill. Then a cone was ready for distribution from his one-man assembly line. One for me, one for Paul, one for Aunt Sue, who reappeared on cue, after taking what I presumed was her first bathroom break in hours, and one for Uncle Mickey. She grabbed her cone and headed to the living room to sit with us. We followed her, waiting to eat our cones over the plastic eating tables which she promptly opened for all three of us, balancing her cone in one hand, tables clutched to her hip with the other.

Unc secured the Breyers box back in its spot in the freezer, and made his way to join us, refilling the scoop his body made in the recliner. He didn't need a folding table, since he already had one permanently opened beside his chair. He always kept the TV guide, his clicker, a hand-grip exerciser, the newspaper—opened to the Jumble—and a sharpened pencil on top. Those were the tools of his retirement-trade, like relics in a museum display. They were mostly boring, tokens of a bygone era, except for the clicker. But sitting next to the other junk on his table, even the clicker looked old. Paul and I crunched our way to a sugar lift. Paul always tried to eat the vanilla from the middle first, saving the chocolate and strawberry for last. Aunt Sue returned to the kitchen to organize food for eternity and we watched whatever Unc clicked on, until the next treat.

Raised during the heart of the Great Depression, Aunt Sue and Uncle Mickey always instructed us to "Save it!" or "Take your time!" while we ate ice cream, drank juice, or partook in any other act of consumption. This was partly confusing to us, as we were always ready to satisfy our taste buds and stomachs. They loved to tell us stories, like one about the holes in their worn-out childhood shoes that had to be covered with cardboard inside until their parents could afford new pairs. We couldn't believe it when they told us they shared a bathroom in the hall of their apartment buildings while growing up. Unlike them, our family had ascended to middle-class economic status by the time Paul and I were kids, so imagining how they grew up with so little was a powerful lesson for me, even as a boy. I remember thinking how unfair it seemed that someone as benevolent as Aunt Sue or someone as responsible and steady as Uncle Mickey had to be hungry at times. *How could they live without having snacks in their cupboard*? I often wondered. We never possessed a mental template for how a hunk of bread, a chunk of provolone, or even Captain Crunch himself might not be there when we summoned him from the cabinet.

Spending time at Aunt Sue's always seemed more fun and more tasty than the activities we did at home, even though the tiles were grimy and the living room sometimes had an "old people smell," as Paul would say. The scent of cutlets frying, or the shows we spent hours watching while Unc snored, his head leaned over the top of his chair, always made us feel like we were someplace important. We could never articulate why, as children, going to their house was so sacred, so entrancing. But Paul and I were always delighted to walk down the block to their house. We knew that "going to Aunt Sue's" was extra special. Sure, it was different from playing ball outside or watching a game, but it was sacred in its own rite, a treat all on its own.

"You're Italian!"

Benvenuto a Casa

As an Italian-American, I have often felt a sense of conflict about my identity. On the one hand, my grandparents, aunts and uncles, and parents instilled a transparent sense of my Italian roots. True to some of the more popular stereotypes, I grew up with a strong sense of value placed on the closeness of the family and neighborhood, the importance of loyalty, a love of food and festivity, and an emphasis on being grateful for what we had, rather than bemoaning what we lacked. While such a foundation was affirming, supportive, close, and often incredibly delicious, I grew up during the height of change within our microcosm of Italian-American culture. Many older relatives were dying, families were branching out from Brooklyn and no longer lived "down the block" from each other, and while the heartbeat of our family still thumped unmistakably Italian, we were quickly learning to be guided less by this rhythm and more by the individualistic, practical, and less overtly passionate American cultural mores. Learning to speak Italian as a child was becoming less common, and the physical connection to Italy was less important as we assimilated into the doings of America.

Growing up in a time of cultural transition gave me the uneasy sense of thinking and feeling in Italian, so to speak, but being expected to act more American. I felt as if I were wearing an invisible emotional restraint. For example, I might have wanted to hug or kiss someone, but I felt compelled instead—mainly through the implications of modeling—to merely say, "Hey, what's up?" Feeling this duality was not the worst thing in the world, although it was a part of an emotional tension—a troubling mental undercurrent—that never waned most of my life. Ironically, it took my first trip to Italy at age thirty-nine to resolve this conflict of the psyche in a beautiful and undoubtedly Italian way.

As our departure neared, my angst about feeling inauthentic continued to haunt me. I began reviewing a college textbook from the one semester of Italian I took twenty years prior, and regretted that I had developed a Spanish proficiency over the years—following the practical wisdom at the time—rather than mastering the musical dance of the Italian cadence. I worried about what my daughters would think when they realized how "un-Italian" I really was compared to those in the motherland. Even more troubling, I feared how the native Italians would perceive me. After all, my father and grandparents—the principals in my life who spoke Italian and seemed most Italian to me—had been gone for many years. I felt their absence more deeply now as I began to reflect on my increasingly withering and distant heritage. While my aforementioned tumult was surely present, so was my excitement about our voyage, especially the opportunity to eat our way through Italy from Venice to Positano. And so we went, my fears and anxieties in tow.

After a dizzying flight from Florida to Venice, we were greeted by a guide awaiting our arrival. After whisking us into a van like diplomats in a Bond movie, the next thing we knew, we were speeding across the Venetian Lagoon—the four of us, my wife and two teen daughters—our belongings bouncing in the waves as our speedboat split the sun on that warm June afternoon. We laughed at each other, feeling a collective sense of joy and travel fatigue. The nature of the moment, we realized, was purely amazing—having flown across the ocean in a 767 through the night—now speeding across Venice to a water drop-off at our first hotel. So far, not a word of English was spoken—except an accidental "thank you" on our part instead of a "grazie" as we parted from our handlers.

Venice was spectacular: the gazillion bridges, the beautiful, old, and timeless art at every corner, the *frescos*, which adorned so many churches, and, of course, the timeless grandeur of St. Mark's Piazza. My fondest Venetian memory, though, came not from any of its myriad historic or architectural landmarks, but at the hands of my daughter Nora playing her flute. We came upon the Rialto Bridge, a famed and scenic central locale where Italians have a sentimental tradition of parting from loved ones "until they meet again" with a customary kiss on each other's cheeks. Nora spontaneously unfolded her music stand at the base of the bridge among a busy crowd of shoppers and passers-by, propped up sheet music for "O Sole Mio," and sounded our happiful arrival in Italy. Her buoyant playing of the traditional anthem in the salty, open air of *Venezia* accepted the ancient city's welcome on our behalf. Imbibed in the sensory appeal of this splendid moment, beginning to absorb Italy *in vivo* for the first time, I hardly focused on my self-centered, "I'm-less-than-Italian" ruminations.

Florence was next. The Uffizi (Italian for "offices," as these buildings once served as such for the city) lined with quaint porticos were striking structures to behold, evoking *Firenze's* former prominence and enduring charm, as were the panoramic views of terra-cotta roofs from the Renaissance-age Pitti Palace balconies. Florentine cuisine was even more captivating than its ancient architecture or famed vistas, demanding our taste buds to acknowledge that we were no longer in Venice, whose lauded fare now seemed almost amateurish in comparison. The pastas were fresh and plentiful, the meat was exceptional, and the cheeses and desserts were divine.

Our first dinner still smells like it happened yesterday. Physically tired from walking much of the city that day, the four of us were greeted by a glorious hunk of beautiful, white, firm Pecorino cheese seconds after taking seats at our much-needed oasis. Pristine and naturally admired all by its perfect lonesome to any human's eyes, an edible Statue of David, the cheese was soon complemented by the warmest, crustiest, and most visually appetizing loaves of bread one could imagine, even in the most creative and indulgent of food fantasies. Already having been delivered to a transcendental state of silent and prayerful reverence for the bounty that lay wonderfully before us, a waiter briefly interrupted our familial trance to add the culinary Holy Spirit to the sacramental table. He drizzled honey—fresh and thick into four mini-plates—with the graceful efficiency of Pope John Paul II conducting Mass, completing this mouth-watering and heartwarming Holy Trinity of Italian delectables. Full of gladness in our hearts, we dutifully commenced with our appropriate responses in the sacred ritual: filling our stomachs.

The only traveling we were required to do on our own was taking the train between cities to meet our next guide and driver. Our next leg to the Amalfi Coast began with a train ride to Naples. This is where the southern connection and magic began.

As we headed south, the train made a few stops, adding more southbound passengers. I found myself noticing that many of their physical features were similar to mine. Of course, most were dark haired and brown-eyed which, while not surprising to me, served as a prelude to the remarkable homogeneity of physical features we would see in the south. The people contrasted with those we'd seen in Venice and Florence. I noticed a few of these passengers also looked at me with a reciprocal sense of familiarity and comfortableness. Our rounder faces and less-than-demure noses made us appear like cousins, as did our relatively forward, friendly, prolonged stares, which usually transformed into mutual smiles before they warmly faded away. It was as if we were saying, "*Buon giorno!*" to each other without uttering a word. Like a boy on a trip to a favorite summer vacation spot, I started to eagerly sense that I was truly heading to where I wanted to be, where I belonged. And that was only the beginning of that enthusiastic sentiment.

After getting picked up in Naples by Pepe, our comical and classically Italian driver who was to bring us to Positano, we were delivered back in time as he promptly and excitedly narrated the beauty of our surroundings.

"*Questo e Vesuvio!*" he uttered with pride and warm jubilance, as we approached Mount Vesuvius, feeling as if we were schoolchildren required to follow our new instructor's prompts.

"*Io sono di Sorrento,*" he continued with bursting pride and vivaciousness, conveying his origin with a happy and nostalgic smile as adorable as it was engaging. I reflected warmly on how the same, old great-aunts and great-uncles my brother G and I enjoyed mocking at family gatherings, would also brag proudly about the Old Country over espresso and Italian cookies. I'm not sure if anyone has more pride about where they're from than an Italian, and Pepe's desire to transmit this to us was unmistakable and no match for the significant language barriers between us.

He brought us to a nice lunch spot en route, overlooking the Bay of Naples. For the first five minutes, he stood shyly a few feet from our table and looked out at the bay, not wanting to impose himself upon our family lunch until we all showed some of our own "Italian-ness" by inviting him to sit and eat with us. For an Italian, such an invitation is more aptly described as an insistence to join, rather than an invitation. Minutes later, he was sucking mussels from their shells and sharing plates with my daughters as if this were a family reunion.

His simple and pure enthusiasm and immediate and easy companionship reminded me of my Nonno, whom my wife and daughters never had the chance to meet. Watching the juice from the mussels slide down Pepe's whiskery, smiling chin, I missed Nonno. As I filled my belly with *pane e olio* and warm provolone chunks, I was also filled with an immediate and robust sense of Italian pride, staring out at the bay and at *Vesuvio*, which bridged the historical gap between Nonno and me. I felt an intimate connection to my grandfather's birthplace of Naples, where it all began for us back in 1890. I began to feel more grateful and more at home than ever.

After checking into a hotel in Positano, which would be our base for the Amalfi Coast leg of the trip, we had our first dinner in the south. It was no accident that meatballs were the catalyst for tears. Two bites in, I realized that they tasted—as the cliché goes—just like Ma's. The tasty tug at my heartstrings from those meatballs and gravy was enough to bring tears to my eyes as I stared out across the dark sea. My daughters asked what was wrong. I had to pause for a few moments before being able to say, "Just a minute," as I still couldn't explain without crying. After gathering myself, I smiled through my glistening eyes and simply said:

"I miss Nonni."

Nonni was what my kids called my mother. My simply pointing to the meatballs was enough for them to make the connection and understand my sentiment. Sensing their shared sadness for me and wanting to quell it, I reassured them that I was fine. Being true to the Italian-American mold I referenced before, I was not comfortable enough to let my vulnerable emotions flow with complete freedom, especially in front of my daughters. And, in truth, I was fine. While I did miss my mother greatly and I was sad in the realization that she had likely made her last trip to Italy years ago, as she was now entering the twilight of her life, I felt some deeper and concurrent feelings of gratitude. I was grateful that I was raised so well by my mom—well enough to miss her in the most basic and profound way—around the act of sitting down with my family for dinner. I also realized that at that moment, with the beauty of my daughters' loving expressions and the starlit sky draping Positano, I felt love at its simplest and deepest. Love for family, love for my roots, and love for something Italians truly know how to relish: the moment. I was happiful and grateful, and, as I had felt many times at Ma's table, "full" in the truest of my senses.

Strolling through Positano that beautiful, balmy evening after dinner, we stopped to look at some street vendors' wares. A middle-aged Italian couple was selling homemade jewelry. They were very friendly and took obvious delight in chatting with passers-by, so the four of us welcomed being next in line to socialize. The woman greeted me, noticing me admiring the Italian horns—a popular superstitious charm thought to protect one from others' *malocchio* (evil eye or hex) worn mostly by men in southern Italy and among Italians in America, especially in the Northeast.

"Where you from?" she asked, in a very Italian manner—forward and genuinely interested—conveying from her tone that she sensed my underlying uneasiness about the topic, or at least about something.

"Well," I started to recite my now-standardized and feeble response, "I lived in New York. My father's family was from the province of Avellino and my mother's from. . ."

"Nahhhh!" she interrupted forcefully, with the comforting stare and assertive reassurance of a seasoned elementary schoolteacher. "You're *Italian*!"

Looking at the distinctly ethnic horn in my hand and into the kind eyes of the knowing woman, who, for a moment, could have been my mom, my favorite, old aunt Assunta, or a dozen other Italian ladies who were distant relatives or neighbors throughout my childhood, I smiled and peacefully acknowledged:

"Si, io sono Italiano."

Nonni

Good with Kids and Dogs

"Here, Ma. I'm putting your Yankees hat on you for a picture. The Yanks need some help against Cleveland tonight," my sister Carmela said loudly as she pointed to the hat, holding it first in front of my mother's face, before slipping it on her eighty-seven-year-old gray and rigid head, as she sat in her wheelchair positioned facing outward from the "alcove" at The Atlantic Care Center on the east end of Long Island, New York.

The alcove—a twelve-by-six-foot cut-out that was perpendicular to the main hallway, where nurses, food servers, and old people walked and wheeled their way by—was the closest thing to a living room or even the bench outside the old house in Brooklyn for my mom these days, and for the last seven years since she has had to live in a residential care facility. She has had Parkinson's for fifteen years and a host of other medical issues that have rendered her almost completely immobile. Her mental faculties have remained exceptionally intact, though, largely due to Carmela's supplemental and incessant micromanagement of the inadequate care provided by The Atlantic, but this was, unfortunately, a bad day on all fronts.

My mom was foggy when I arrived that afternoon from California, confused about who was who, including my daughter Victoria, who also had come into town to visit from Massachusetts. Things had not been going well recently. She had been hospitalized twice for infections of one kind or another, and some hallucinatory behavior had started. She would repeatedly eat an imaginary piece of chocolate cake. We thought she might be dying soon and were there to make our final goodbyes.

As I took Ma's picture in her Yankees cap with the interlocking N and Y, she lit up momentarily. There was likely no better item that could have ignited her awareness than that iconic symbol of our family history. With a heavy heart, I imagined her wearing a Yankees cap, as she did, on her way to deliver me almost fifty years earlier on a cold February night in Brooklyn, and how life had now come full circle. I hid the emerging tears behind my iPhone as I fiddled with what would become my latest Facebook profile picture seconds later, an homage to Ma and a hopeful catalyst for the Yanks.

They lost the opening game of a best-of-five playoff series to the Indians that night. Like Ma seemed to us that day, their bats were asleep, almost unrecognizable to anyone who followed them, as they limped their way to a dreary defeat. Among Carmela, Victoria and me, there was an eerie sense in the living room of the Sag Harbor Airbnb house we had rented for the week as the Yanks' lethargy compounded the pervasive sadness around my mom's fading health. I knew it was going to be a difficult week. Quickly shutting off the TV before the postgame show to further prevent salt being rubbed into the wound of the Yankees' loss that night, I realized that it simply wasn't going to be OK to lose my mom.

The following day was a blitzkrieg of unsettling emotions. The doctors had recently decided that my mother's risk of aspiration was too high if she were to continue to drink regular, non-thickened liquids, like water, so she was restricted to thickened liquids. Doing so was distasteful for her and she took hours each day to ingest enough teaspoons of the gelatinous goo to hydrate her. Even more troubling was the fact that the aides who were supposed to ensure that she consumed enough goo were continually failing to do so. So, my mother would frequently become dehydrated, and, if it weren't for my sister "sneaking" Ma cups of water, she likely would have been dead already.

Essentially, The Atlantic created a situation where my mother could survive only if we took matters into our own hands, and the chasm between my mom's needs and the care she received only widened as she became less able to adequately articulate her aches, pains, and the events surrounding her treatment to them and us. We forced a meeting with the head administrator of the facility that day.

"Hello, Frank," Carmela began with a polite sternness as Frank entered his office with a visible look of surprised concern.

"Hello, Carmela. I thought just you and I were meeting today," he replied, with a discernible tone of defensiveness and unease.

"We are," said Carmela, returning serve. "And I brought my brother Silvio and his daughter Victoria, too. Is that all right?" Carmela added sarcastically, knowing that it was far from all right with Frank.

We all shook hands with him with obligatory discomfort before commencing our "progress meeting."

"So," Victoria began, uninvited. "I think what's still confusing me is the lack of liquids my grandmother receives in a day. It sounds like you have a wonderful plan thought out here, but we keep arriving each day to find that she hasn't been given any water. Can you see where I might feel a little lost here?" my daughter asked, using her kind teacher voice, leading the incompetent administrator to the answer.

"Oh, well, we can start a log of her liquids. And it doesn't *have* to be just water. We give her hot chocolate, too." he answered, crossing his arms and fiddling with the stupid gold hoop in his ear.

"Hot chocolate?" Victoria queried, sounding surprised. "For hydration?"

"Absolutely." he said, fiddling away, refusing to look into her eyes.

"So..." she said, looking up and continuing to talk to him as if he were one of her six-year-old cousins who she was convincing to eat fruit instead of cookies for a snack. "This is amazing to hear, because I have this huge water bottle that I'm always filling with water to try and stay hydrated. But, you're telling me that I can actually fill it with hot chocolate?"

He paused, avoiding the direct gaze coming from the 5-foot granddaughter who was not in the mood to play anymore.

"Yes. Hot chocolate provides just as much hydration as water."

"Wow!" she exclaimed. "Could you show me some sort of documentation of that? I'm so excited to switch up my regimen."

"Um, it's pretty common knowledge. Just ask any doctor." he answered quickly, annoyed.

"I'll be sure to do that." she said, smiling sweetly.

"Another quick question," I interjected, "Who should I speak to if I were unhappy or unclear about some of the procedures under your auspices? And, as my daughter asked, why no reply on the emails? Are you actually receiving them or is there perhaps a server issue we could look into? I have a background in digital marketing and I know sometimes emails can get misdirected…"

Carmela sat quietly, allowing her piercing stare at Frank to do her talking. While the veins in her neck bulged intensely, as they seemed to incessantly do whenever she did battle at The Atlantic, I could also see some relief in the cross-armed stance she maintained, appreciative that today, she had two reinforcements relieving her of the front-line duty she tirelessly undertook.

Frank stammered and winced at the triple-piranha onslaught, feeling the tingling sense of pain from all angles, and feebly replying, "Well, as far as who you would go to if you weren't happy with how the care for your mother is going, maybe if you aren't satisfied with the level of care..."

"Are you going there so quickly, Frank? Really?" I interrupted coolly and with a mocking sense of surprise, letting him know that we weren't going to buckle that easily at the implied threat of moving my mother to another facility at this stage of the game.

"We can get to that consideration perhaps at another time, Frank," I added. "In the meantime, though, would I go to your boss if I had concerns? And what about the emails surrounding the neglect incident? And the failure to execute on thickened liquids, which shouldn't even be given to Maria in the first place? Let's talk about those issues—in any order you prefer."

"Is your personal boss still Abe Miller, Frank?" Carmela chimed in. "My mother met him personally once when he was visiting the facility, long before you were here."

Looking suddenly as if he were suddenly trying to swallow a whole cup of thickened liquids at once, he sputtered in response, "Well, Abe is still one of the owners, yes, but you would go to the State if you had a complaint."

"You would prefer that I make a formal complaint with *The State,* Frank, rather than go to your boss?" I inquired with a puzzled tone.

"Well, that's just who you would go to," Frank hiccupped his way through a response, seeming to further drown with each word.

An hour later and with the prospect now introduced that perhaps this conversation might have been recorded thus far on someone's cell phone, and with Victoria noting casually that Abe Miller's Facebook page looked "really interesting" as she fiddled with her phone, Frank's tone and collaborative thinking began to improve greatly.

Still, despite my intimidation, Carmela's overwhelming amount of evidence of negligence from The Atlantic Care Facility, Victoria's insistent questioning, and ultimately more meetings with the actual owner of the nursing home, we did not leave feeling good about the care my mom would continue to receive.

The Yankees faced similarly tough odds that evening in their second game against Cleveland, when the best pitcher in the league was slated to give the Indians a two-games-to-none advantage. The early innings surprised many as the Yanks bombarded the Indians ace and amassed an 8–3 early lead. We welcomed the emotional boost as we watched with surprised elation. Exhausted, defeated, and angry, Carmela, Victoria, and I dared to rally with the Yanks as we watched around the TV, eating anchovy pizza, feeling cautiously optimistic, knowing, but refusing to acknowledge, that we were putting too much stake in this game. We needed a win.

Not today. Faltering badly, the Yanks gave up their five-run lead and eventually lost the game in extra innings. It was almost sure to be a deadly blow for their season hopes as they now faced a two-game deficit in the best-of-five playoff series. I quickly shut off the TV. Carmela went home. I turned away, trying to swallow the anchovy in my mouth. I had felt more than my share of emotionally numbing tough losses throughout my decades of irrational attachment to the Yankees, but this was one of the worst I could remember. The welcomed and euphoric distraction of an apparent improbable win just a short while ago disappeared, settling instead into a heavy pain in my chest and stomach. The ache was worsened by the impaired digestion of three slices of pizza, which I had habitually and frantically medicated myself with in the middle innings. I felt even worse for Victoria. She had trekked away from her newly begun Ph.D. program to see her Nonni, only to ride a jarring and multipronged emotional roller-coaster, which now included the Yanks.

As my mom did many times through the years when the Yanks dealt us an emotional blow, worse for her as such losses often meant increasing financial woes due to her husband's careless gambling on them, we did the only thing we knew how to do. We shared a few empty rationalizations about the game in a futile attempt to lessen the emotional blow, sucked it up and went to sleep. On to the next day.

Like a well-watered plant that was previously neglected to an apparent point of no return, my mom perked up over the next couple of days to our grateful amazement. Her sudden astuteness and beaming clarity reminded me of a scene from the movie *Awakenings*, where patients receiving certain medications promptly emerged from catatonic states of unawareness and rigidity after years of being written off. In this case, though, my mother was simply given water and proper attention. While the ongoing battle with The Atlantic was only beginning, especially since her revival only strengthened the merits of our grievances, today was a day best spent simply visiting Ma, enjoying and revering the moments of happiful interaction among us, moments we weren't sure we would ever experience again just a day earlier. My mom's dear friend Anne, 100 years old and full of a lifetime of old-school Irish piss and vinegar, barked wryly upon seeing my mom acting like her old self.

"Where ya' been?" Anne said, prodding her with a poke in the shoulder as she wheeled up next to her.

"On a little vacation," my mother quipped in return, to the delight of us all. Seeing them joust affectionately was an exclamation point on the notion that Ma's rally was actual and not just a product of our collective wishful thinking. Seeing an opportunity to maximize Ma's improved condition, a highly specialized skill that Carmela had mastered over the years of taking care of her, Carmela produced a ready-made salad from her bag. As usual, the salad was stocked with arugula, infinite balls of mozzarella, olives (with the pits, so Carmela could unnoticeably assess Ma's chewing and swallowing abilities as she ate them), enough olive oil for a week for most, and a massive chunk of Italian bread (packed separately, of course, so it wouldn't get soggy).

Carmela methodically fed Ma the salad, which acted like sunlight to the now-watered plant that was my mom, simultaneously peppering her with questions and reflective statements in order to both assess how aware she was of recent events, and to help her focus and prepare to get the most out of today's activities. Carmela had become a master at this empathetic and highly efficient multitasking, which just minutes later produced a satiated, well-briefed and ready-for-action eighty-seven-year-old. I felt a vicarious sense of contentedness, as if I myself had just eaten that soul-soothing salad, simply knowing that my mom was herself today. I mostly watched family members engage with her for the rest of the afternoon. It was unseasonably warm, so we sat in the outdoor courtyard for hours.

My brother Joseph, who lived locally, arrived from the airport with my daughter Nora, who had just flown in from college in Alabama. She was thrilled to see her Nonni as she usually saw her—happy, buoyant, and funny—rather than a shadow of herself, as Nora had been cautioned to expect just yesterday.

The Yankees had a homecoming, too, as they welcomed the Indians for the first of two potential games. We were hoping they would at least throw a counterpunch before likely fading for the year. They did squeak out a win by a 1–0 margin keeping their post-season chances on life support and our spirits up, too. It was a good day.

The next few days were thankfully less traumatic as Ma continued to improve. I visited her daily and spent a few meditative mornings and relaxing evenings in my favorite village on Earth, Sag Harbor, New York. As I walked a mile into town one morning from the beautifully renovated old home I had rented, my heart and mind filled with enthusiastic warmth and excitement. I have always felt that way in Sag Harbor, from the first years my family discovered it when I was a child. Something about the glistening light from the surrounding bays, the bustle of this old, whalers' town intrigued and captivated me with its rough-and-crusty past serving as the backdrop for a modern gem of Americana. Amid its haunting beauty and charm, I reminisced about jumping into nearby ocean waves, days listening to Yankee games on the radio at Long Beach, frisbee catches, barbeques, and horseshoes. I even spent one summer alone out there at seventeen, old enough to wade in some risky waters, yet still too young to safely navigate their treacherous tides. I love this town so much that I don't mind my five-dollar, extra-shot lattes these days, and especially not this week visiting Ma.

As I meandered around the oval Main Street this morning, I sat on my mom's bench—located prominently with a lifetime, engraved plaque Carmela had bought from the town in her honor. "Maria Carmela DiCristo—Good with Kids and Dogs." There could never be a bench big enough to encompass the pages of things my mom was good at. I laughed aloud, recalling how my mom persuaded the town to reposition half of the benches to face the storefronts, thus allowing people sitting on those benches the option to watch others going by and the storefronts, rather than just the traffic in the street—such a practical, considerate, and intelligent idea, and one that focused on the enrichment of experience for others. How apropos, I reflected, with an unabashed smile and quiet pride at my mother's humble and beautiful contribution.

I sat on her bench, crying joyful tears, as I pondered the inspiring truth about what an amazing person my mother was, and why she was one of the principal reasons I loved Sag Harbor so dearly. I replayed images of those sacred summers, which went from good to great because of my mom's presence: how the beach days were extra special because of Ma's pepperoni sandwiches on Italian bread; the scrumptious dinners at Conca with massive eggplant parm heroes, which I could hardly hold in my little hands; and how just being out in sunny Sag Harbor was even warmer and more comforting because of my mom.

I continued to sit on her bench in awe of my mother's lifetime of staggering resilience. She was born in the heart of the Great Depression, and lost her own mother at age three to a routine surgery that went bad. She had a corrupt father, whose main attachment to her as a child revolved around using her as a pawn of sympathy to the underworld figures to whom he was indebted. After a string of good years and raising five children, she lost her life's love when she was just fifty-seven (and was left with nothing material, except his debt), then unnaturally lost her first son less than a year later when he was killed at just thirty-one. On top of all that, I remembered how she felt compelled to detach from the vestiges of extended family that remained in the city after they narcissistically claimed to feel "abandoned" from her move east to Sag Harbor. Hers was a journey of survival, though, to collect the pieces of her broken heart and reinvent herself.

She quickly became a known and welcomed presence in town, weaving herself into Sag Harbor's rich and diverse cultural fabric. Part-time innkeeper and de facto representative of one of the most beautiful places on the planet, all without ever driving a car.

Then, another one of her sons decided that it was "unfortunate that family, unlike friends, couldn't be chosen," as he rationalized his complete detachment from his nuclear family, including our mother. He became dead to her while still alive, another handful of salt in her numerous wounds. The weight of these unfortunate truths weighed suddenly heavy on my mind as I sat alone, save for my mom's living epitaph embossed in the wood plank behind my shoulder.

The melancholy mood was only momentary, though. Following my mom's lifelong example of remaining upbeat, accepting and possessing a remarkably genuine slant toward the kind of optimism normally reserved for fables, I smiled and felt a booming pride. She lived a happy life and was still doing so. She approached her obstacles with zeal, fortitude, and strength, knowing somehow that she would persevere and nudge whoever needed nudging along with her in the same resilient direction. She never succumbed to difficulties, despite having well more than a lifetime's worth, so why should I on her behalf? After all, I was one of those who had benefited most from her steady and uplifting approach to life. Even now, as Ma took her final swings at life, she rallied herself forward with a divine spirit and enthusiasm that was still carrying us—her children—upward in her wake.

The Yanks had a parallel message of their own for Cleveland that night in the Bronx. Not so fast. We're not done yet. Yankee bats thundered to a 7–3 victory. Like my mom, they were beating the odds, going the distance and forcing one more game.

Victoria was back in Massachusetts the next day, I in California, Nora in Alabama, and the Yankees in Cleveland. One more tip of the cap from the Bronx Bombers was in the cards. In the second drubbing of Cleveland's best hurler in just days, the Yankees took a page out of Ma's book, reminding us of the inspirational and contagious power of hope and resiliency.

We had no idea how well she would continue to fare, but we knew we had done what we could to help her, and that Carmela would resume carrying the heavy, yet well-lit, torch from here. We also knew that Nonni was fine today and that she would remain so until the end. And so would we.

Boston Lisa

A Date to Remember

"So, you really aren't gonna tell me your name? All I have to go on is your Match username, BostonStrong? What should I call you until I'm so gifted with such sensitive information? Forget that question; I'll just call you 'Boston' for now. Even though it's hard for me to even say that word without having sudden, unhappiful thoughts about a certain group of red-uniformed men, whom I have despised since I could say the word 'Yankees'." And that's how our flirtatious banter began on our first phone call in May of 2018, hours after e-meeting on Match.

I typically dismissed women who employed such unusual and evasive communication tactics in a New York minute. I had become savvy enough by now to surmise that such covert beginnings signaled any number of potential booby traps, such as still being married, hiding from a volatile ex (sometimes both), or extreme emotional brokenness not nearly healed enough to be dating.

Something about Boston, though—well, I guess several things about her really—intrigued my intuition and steered my thinking right out of its reliably comfortable box. Already feeling the full-bodied pulse of liking her, even just from chatting on the phone, I decided to play along with her anonymity ploy. I had to give her a shot. As it turned out, Lisa texted me her name just after we hung up and playfully ended the mystery.

We met the next night, beginning with a drink, overlooking the Pacific from one of the most scenic vantages in Newport Coast. Lisa had requested meeting somewhere we could catch the sunset while we chatted before going to dinner. I happily obliged, appreciative that she didn't need to play things that safe by meeting in the sterile, over-lit, over-crowded, boisterous environs of a coffee shop, as many women prefer initially. By now, I had stopped agreeing to go on dates in coffee shops altogether, understanding that a woman's reluctance to "risk" committing herself to ninety minutes over a meal provided me with more insight about her than an entire battery of psychological tests ever could.

"That charm," Lisa said, pointing to the multicolored Italian horn dangling from the gold necklace around my neck, then reaching over to lift it a few inches off my chest, as if to clarify that she was not referring to the invisible charm next to it.

"So, you just totally own being Italian, then?"

I was turned on by her targeted line of inquiry and refreshing strength, directness, and enthusiasm surrounding her question. Her bright-green eyes shimmered and eagerly fixed upon me, anticipating confirmation of my Italian-ness. I slowly unwrapped a full grin, channeling DeNiro instinctively and delivering one of his classic, head-slanting, eye-shifting, idiosyncratic facial tilts.

"Yeah, you could say that," I said, peering back into the now-widened gates of her Emerald City. Noticing that the sun had almost disappeared beyond the ocean, I pointed to our side and reminded her to look. She barely glanced at the picturesque scene to her left, darting her head back toward me instead and offering the sun a mere conciliatory nod.

"Yeah, that's nice," she said, smiling at me. From my vantage, what felt "nice" was having this fun, five-foot-seven, Boston beauty leave the sun on the horizon for me.

It was no coincidence that my chosen route for the fifteen-minute drive to NK's Bistro wound us through the perfect sunset road. Day surrendered beautifully to night as we transitioned from the sunset vista to the cozy, leather seats of my Acura. I drove with my left hand on the wheel and instinctively clasped her hand in mine with my right, both resting atop her left thigh. I realized then (less than seventy-five minutes after two Easts met out West) how potent and exhilarating natural chemistry could feel. Her hand was supposed to be in mine, and we both knew it. I had never experienced that feeling, at least not since I watched my first crush read my love poem thirty-seven years earlier. Following a sacred sense of thrill and immediate compatibility, we then engaged in the kind of personal revelations that most couples balk at doing after fifteen years, no less during the first fifteen minutes alone with each other. The normal and tired restraints of first-date protocols vanished with the fading daylight, succumbing to the night's divine forces. Our new connection was magnetic.

I knew as I parked my car at NK's (the car now feeling more like our private heavenly chariot) that tonight's experience at my favorite bistro would soon relegate all my previous engagements there to a distant spot in the backseat of my mind. I beamed over at Lisa before we exited the car, paused a few seconds as our hearts adjusted to the shared and still-amplifying euphoria.

"We should just kiss now already," I suggested.

"I was thinking the same thing." she echoed sweetly through a heavenly smile and green-eyed beam, leaning in to meet my lips and seal our fate.

Gliding into NK's hand in hand a few minutes later, my mind drifted among its clouds. I reflected happifully on how this moment with Lisa felt as fun, sacred, and more free than any of the numerous dates I'd been on since moving to California. My imagination, guided by a down-to-earth acknowledgment of how outer-worldly this union already was, played our script forward. I wondered if one of my life's deepest longings was, in fact, right before my eyes. Sensing that surreal and enthusiastic possibility, an even-deeper intuition guided me in that moment. I understood that everything about my connection to Lisa was perfect and beautiful, and that simply feeling and acknowledging the divine chemistry of the moment was all that mattered. Pausing our steps and turning her toward me, I gazed into her soft, welcoming green eyes, and said:

"I'm glad we're here right now."

My Sweet Lord!

Epilogue

AND an old priest said, "Speak to us of Religion."

And he said:

Have I spoken this day of aught else?

Is not religion all deeds and all reflection,

And that which is neither deed nor reflection, but a wonder and a surprise ever springing in the soul, even while the hands hew the stone or tend the loom?

Who can separate his faith from his actions, or his belief from his occupations?

Who can spread his hours before him, saying,

"This for God and this for myself;

"This for my soul and this other for my body"?

All your hours are wings that beat through space from self to self.

He who wears his morality but as his best garment were better naked.

The wind and the sun will tear no holes in his skin.

And he who defines his conduct by ethics imprisons his song-bird in a cage.

The freest song comes not through bars and wires.

And he to whom worshipping is a window, to open but also to shut, has not yet visited the house of his soul whose windows are from dawn to dawn.

Your daily life is your temple and your religion.

Whenever you enter into it take with you your all.

Take the plough and the forge and the mallet and the lute,

The things you have fashioned in necessity or for delight.

For in reverie you cannot rise above your achievements nor fall lower than your failures.

And take with you all men:

For in adoration you cannot fly higher than their hopes nor humble yourself lower than their despair.

And if you would know God, be not therefore a solver of riddles.

Rather look about you and you shall see Him playing with your children.

And look into space; you shall see Him walking in the cloud, outstretching His arms in the lightning and descending in rain.

You shall see Him smiling in flowers, then rising and waving His hands in trees.

—Khalil Gibran, *The Prophet*

Every day when driving to work, I pass the same pool where the redemptive fires of SALutations! first ignited my soul almost five years prior. Running late one May morning in 2018, I realize that I forgot to engage in my daily practice of prayer and meditation before leaving my home. Forgivingly, and free of the heavy laments that used to weigh down my spirit at even the slightest miscue, I smile at God and myself, shunning the now nearly inaudible taunts of Screwtape, and decide to improvise my normal ritual with an on-wheels version today. Deferring the soothing sounds of The Coffee House radio station for the moment, I make the sign of the cross and initiate my daily plug-in with The Spirit while rolling slowly out of the neighborhood.

Thank you, God, for what I have. Thank you for saving me, and for my life. I conclude, feeling grateful and satisfied.

The drive to work takes only about six minutes, but this morning's clock would be set to divine time, concerning itself not with such earthly notions as minutes or days, deadlines or traffic. I press the audio button and hear the start of one of the most spiritually delicious songs I know, "My Sweet Lord" by George Harrison.

Some people have described the sensation of seeing their lives "flash before them" during near death experiences. I am now being bathed in the light of my wonderful life—with images of hundreds of people and thousands of experiences simultaneously present. While I drive to work in my black, earthly sedan, God delivers the final installment of my soul back to itself via this heavenly detour. George Harrison replaces George Bailey, serving as the divine Clarence of my transition, infusing me with God's joy through this sacred musical bridge.

"My sweet Lord..." Harrison sings. I smile at G, knowing that our hearts are closer now than ever. I send love to Kathy, grateful for our daughters and our past life together. I cry with peaceful happifulness at Victoria and Nora. I thank God for Kundalini's tap on my Western shoulder.

"*Sat Nam,*" I utter. I feel deep love for the Jews in my old neighborhood and thank them for acknowledging my remorse. I feel reverence for the Catholicism of my youth, touching my father's gold crucifix around my neck and thanking it for the beautiful guardrails of conscience, which still set my moral compass. I briefly hear the faint call of Screwtape for me to impugn this flawed religion for its grossly human imperfections. I smile in return, tuning instead into George's rhythmic and deeper truths.

"Hallelujah..." I hear the chorus exalt. I know as sure as my heart beats that Gibran's words about religion are infallible, that I don't have to explain, defend, debate, or even speak aloud of God's truth within me to another human and that I am now *living* in truth, a far more potent and honest force of instruction than any formal dogma could ever offer. I feel sad in my heart for those who snuffed out my brother and stuffed his pulseless remains into a trunk, no longer angry at them or in need of proclaiming an elaborately justified and Screwtape-tainted stance of righteous indignation on the matter. I now understand that my "indignation" was an act of prideful protection of my once-shattered heart.

"I really wanna see you, Lord, but it takes so long, my Lord..." the music continues to fill my car and my heart. I send more love to Kathy, and identify the palpable sentiments of Elizabeth Gilbert's transformative journey in *Eat, Pray, Love,* as she disembarked from the mangled attachments to her ex. The voices of criticism and anger that have echoed so loudly in my ears and heart are silent. I am ecstatic again that I threw the ringer forty-two years ago. I sing aloud with George and acknowledge the fact that I share music with Nora these days and not fishing poles.

"Hare Krishna, Krishna Krishna..." we sing.

I raise an imaginary toast to the women who helped center my East and West, sending warmth and thankfulness to them all, recalling the snipes of their own brokenness, the fibs of age-related angst, their gestures of pure love, and many other female doings and undoings that had involved me, as they are now revealed in their beautiful sameness. They, like I, were wading in the shared and choppy waters of truth in search of their own oases. I see Lisa's beaming smile and inviting green-eyed stare, and I feel pleased in the knowledge that I have finally found the right haystack, even perhaps the elusive needle. I feel soothed by the full knowledge that my spirit is amply nourished and perfectly whole in divine union *with itself.*

"My, my, my Lord..." fills my car and my soul.

I arrive at my office building and habitually lower my window to swipe my parking card, granting myself access to the lot and a moment to transition back to Earth. Heaven's instruments usher my soul into its new position of understanding as my car seems to drive itself into its parking space.

"I really wanna see you Lord but it takes so long my Lord. OOOO My Lord," I pray. I make no effort to clear the joyful tears from my face, and spend a few moments attempting to catalog this celestial morning gift through a voice memo on my phone. I know that such languages of the heart could have no proper earthly translation, but I persist anyway, needing to always remember this moment, no matter how dimmed or muted my earthly lens becomes. This is too sacred.

I recall Clarence's parting salutation to George on that wonderfully fateful Christmas Eve night, "No man is a failure who has friends." And in a nod to my principal editor and daughter-in-chief, and to the divinity within us all, I reflect, *Yeah, no PERSON is a failure who has friends, and for this, I too, have a wonderful life.*

ABOUT THE AUTHOR

Sal Guarino is from Brooklyn, New York. He has been a mental health counselor, educator, digital marketing expert, and life coach. He also spent time working in the spirited worlds of Wall Street and the automotive industry. Could he wave a magic wand, he'd spend all his time on his most beloved pursuits: communing with his two adult daughters, life-coaching and mentoring, dining, story-telling, and singing a cappella standards.

Sal's current pursuits include writing additional books, conducting team building workshops for businesses, and consulting in the digital marketing arena.

Most of all, Sal cherishes what he has been able to glean from these diverse opportunities: a daily sense of gratitude, beauty, and enthusiasm. Sal lives in Newport Beach, California.

This is his first book.